Cultural China

我的媽媽是精靈

My Mother is a Fairy

Danyan Chen

Better Link Press

This book is edited and designed by the Editorial Committee of *Cultural China* series

Managing Editors: Naiqing Xu, Youbu Wang, Ying Wu
Project and Executive Editor: Ying Wu
Editors: Sue Hill, Peter Zhang, Kexi Zhou

Story by Danyan Chen
Translation by J. J. Jiang
Interior and Cover Design: Yinchang Yuan, Wenqing Xue

ISBN-13: 978-1-60220-202-3
ISBN-10: 1-60220-202-8

Address any comments about *My Mother is a Fairy* to:

Better Link Press
99 Park Ave
New York, NY 10016
USA
or
Shanghai Press and Publishing Development Company
F 7 Donghu Road, Shanghai, China (200031)
Email: comments_betterlinkpress@hotmail.com

Computer typeset by Yuan Yinchang Design Studio, Shanghai
Printed in China by Shanghai Donnelley Printing Co. Ltd.

1   2   3   4   5   6   7   8   9   10

CONTENTS

Chapter I
Something Earth-shaking Happened at My Home

An earthshaking event is usually preceded by another uneventful day. At least that's my experience.

One evening, Dad sat near the table reading the evening newspaper. Our mailbox was so small that the postman had to crimp the paper to cram it into the box. "Tomorrow, we must install a new mailbox," Dad said every time he peeled open a page from crumple. But Dad was too lazy, and he never did it.

Mom emerged from the kitchen with the dishes she prepared for the dinner. Tonight the main dish was mushroom fried with sliced pork, and the latter was quivering on top of the dish as Mom carried it to the table. "Dinner will be ready in a minute," she told me, "but you can eat first. The fried mushroom will be good for you, and you can run faster than a rabbit in your next PE class. Rabbits don't have fried mushrooms."

I never liked mealtime because I never felt hungry. Tonight, however, I couldn't wait. So, I helped set the table. Mom was in a rush trying to finish her illustrations for the book "Red and Black" that afternoon, so she was late getting to the kitchen. I had to finish my dinner before I was allowed to watch the TV series "Growing Pains".

Besides textbooks, the series was something all my classmates shared. Like many others, I most liked the prelude of each episode: photos stacked together one by one, showing a baby growing into a man. Even the parents in the TV series grew up like that. We yearned to grow up quickly, so we wouldn't have to sit in the classroom bored to tears. I liked this TV series so much that I had even become a shutterbug. On my birthday, Dad and Mom gave me a point-and-shoot camera. After that, I was always taking pictures though I didn't know much about photography. I couldn't explain, for example, why the pictures I took of Mom were invariably hazy and she never cast a shadow, while photos of my classmates always came out quite clear.

I poured some wine for Dad. He was a surgeon, supporting Mom and me by cutting open people with a scalpel. Everyday he came home from work looking dog tired. He never used his keys. He even never bothered to grope for his keys. He just banged on the door. Walking into the house, he always wore the look of a man being crucified. Dad always had a glass of rice wine at dinner. As soon as the alcohol coursed through his body and his face reddened, Dad seemed rejuvenated. He read the evening newspaper very thoroughly. He even read the missing-persons bulletin tucked away in page corners, as if he wanted to find some information about a missing member of his own family.

He sat in his special rocking chair, forcefully rocking back and forth. It creaked as it rocked. Dad would tell Mom what he saw in the newspaper and she would add a few words. When Dad denounced a property advertisement in the paper as misleading, Mom would say, "When the ad says it's only five minutes away from the Metro station, it actually means the time it would take to fly there." Mom usually made such off-hand remarks when she was in a rush to finish an illustration. She was a freelance artist, working at home.

There were three cups on the table. Rice wine for Dad, Sprite for me and Coca-Cola for Mom. I wasn't allowed to drink Coke yet because I wasn't 16. Mom said there was something in the Coke that would stick to the teeth of a child and turn them black. She said girls should not have black teeth. In ancient China, women all had black teeth and that was why they always used their hands to cover their mouths when they grinned. Every time Mom expounded this line, Dad would immediately tell her to stop talking nonsense.

Despite her theories about dental repercussions, Mom loved Coke and always drank it with meals. For dinner, each of us had our own chair and our own cup.

I was filling them as usual when I suddenly realized that I had inadvertently switched Dad's and Mom's cups. I had poured some of Dad's rice wine into Mom's cup. I knew Mom never drank alcohol; she wouldn't even eat the special dish called drunken shrimps, made with rice wine. I looked at the golden-brownish wine at the bottom of Mom's cup. It looked harmless enough. I was preoccupied with wanting to eat in time to catch the prelude to "Growing Pains". I sneaked a sip of wine from Mom's cup, and did not find much wine taste in it. It was not very different from the Chinese medicine flavor in the Coke.

Dad had looked up from his newspaper. "Chen Miaomiao, don't steal your mother's Coke. Your teeth will turn black."

I was startled at the harshness of his tone.

Mom heard his words and yelled out from the kitchen: "Chen Miaomiao, don't drink my Coke."

A child's soul is easily scared out of his/her body. As I was flustered by the scolding, the Coke in my hand rushed into the cup. I will be more careful next time, I thought. Still feeling guilty about the whole episode, I put the big bottle of Coca-Cola next to Mom's cup, hoping that would make everything seem normal.

Then Mom brought the rice to the table and sat down. She always sat at the farthest end of the table from my father because he reeked of wine by dinnertime. Mom took a sip of her Coke.

Right away she turned pale. With the Coke still in her mouth, she pushed away from the table and jumped to her feet. Her eyes opened wide. She looked at Dad in panic and then spit it out.

Dad jumped up from his chair and lurched forward to grab hold of her. Mom's body fell gently into his arms, where she hung like a piece of weightless silk. As Dad carried her toward their bedroom, I saw Mom's legs floating in the air like corners of a silk dress flapping gently in a breeze.

Then I noticed something odd. Her feet were slowly turning blue. I was flabbergasted. It looked like something out of science fiction. I thought I should rush up and help support Mom's feet, but I was too scared. Then a red cloth slipper slid off one of her blue feet and dropped to the floor in front of me. I screamed, terrifying even myself with the piercing sound of my own voice.

Dad carried Mom into their bedroom. Under the dim light, I saw Mom's face was also turning blue. It was so light, so thin and swaying. In the next moment, it vanished as if covered by a piece of blue cloth. Mom's face seemed to fade away, leaving her a blue shadow. Dad carefully laid her on the bed and covered her with a quilt.

I dared not move any closer; neither did I want to stay too far behind by myself. I looked back at the table and saw a white wisp of steam rising from Mom's rice bowl. It imagined Mom would soon rise in an apparition of steam. I grabbed a corner of Dad's shirt and pressed myself tightly against his back. My heart was thumping and I felt cold. I saw Mom's hands. They still looked as slender as before. But they were blue now and clenched tightly.

"Don't be afraid, Chen Miaomiao," Dad said, holding one of my hand. His hand was very cold and clammy.

"What's wrong with her?"

"She must have taken some wine. She should not drink wine," Dad said.

"Is she drunk?" I asked. "Let's rush her to the hospital."

Dad held me and looked at me for a long moment. Then he spoke. "Chen Miaomiao, don't be afraid," he said. "Today you have discovered our family secret and you should never tell this to anyone. Your Mom is not a real human being."

Mom not a real human being? Then what was she? I was stunned and baffled.

"She is another kind of being, other than human. Ours is a very large world."

"Are you saying that Mom is a ghost?"

The image of Casper came into my mind, but that was just an animated movie. That wasn't real. But me, I was real. I was a student at the Primary School attached to the Shanghai No. 1 Teachers' School. How could I see ghosts?

"Another kind of being," Dad said, correcting my reference to ghosts. "Another kind of human being." Then he tightly held my hands. "You needn't be afraid. She would never hurt you. She is not the kind of ghost you are thinking about."

"Then what is she?" I asked.

"Another kind of human being that belongs to another space. Our world is like a beehive and there are many holes. Different human beings live in different holes. Mom is the human being from another hole. They don't hurt our form of human beings. Has your Mom ever hurt you?"

"But she looked just like a real human being," I said, recalling her normal image in my mind.

"But she's not real human. Look!" Dad raised his hand to point to Mom, and the little wind stirred up by the motion of his sleeve made Mom's body flutter in the air. Dad rushed to close the door and windows to prevent her from being blown away.

She was so light. Luckily, she was under a heavy quilt. She was just like a hydrogen air balloon covered by a quilt.

It was me who made the awful blunder that had caused this. Dad said alcohol was Mom's bane. Once she touched or even smelled it, she would immediately betray herself.

The door and windows of their bedroom were all tightly closed, but I felt a kind of chill there that I had never experienced before. It was like a cold draft emitted when the door of a refrigerator was opened. The chill was coming from Mom's bed. There was also a sort of sweet, fishy smell that made me feel sick to my stomach. Mom was like a piece of ice emitting a strange odor.

Dad's body was very warm. I leaned against his soft stomach while he held my hands.

"Did she give birth to me?" I asked.

"Yes," said Dad.

"Then, am I a human or a blue human?" I asked, fearing to hear the response.

Dad answered: "Thank heavens, you are a real human child."

He looked at me. His eyes were enlarged behind his glasses. They were so big and the black pupils were staring straight into me. I wondered what more horrifying secrets my father had to tell me.

I looked back hard at him. What if Dad wasn't a real human, either? He knew everything. And if I didn't ask, he wouldn't tell me anything. How would I know he was not a blue man?

I screamed and jumped away from him, in the process losing my balance and falling into Mom's bed. I didn't feel as though I was crashing into anything, but as my body hit, I heard a very feeble groan from beneath the quilt. It sounded like the woeful mew of a kitten in distress.

I was aware of the cold and the fishy, earthy smell that reminded me of the time Li Yuchen and I killed an earthworm. I leapt up and ran out of the room. A large shadow loomed behind me. It was Dad.

I screamed again. Dad caught hold of me from behind. His body was warm. "I'm not a blue man," he shouted. "I'm not a blue man. Like you, I am a real human. We are real human beings."

We walked back into the lounge. Shaken, I pointed to the wine bottle on the table. "Drink it," I said, surprised by the force of my demand. "Drink it to prove you are real."

Dad took a swig from the bottle. Almost immediately, his face turned red. He was not a blue man, certainly not. Then, I remembered that Dad always drank rice wine every evening and never turned blue.

I wanted to drink the wine, too. I wanted to prove that I too was a real human. Anticipating my thoughts, Dad handed me the bottle. "Take a sip," he said. "Don't be afraid. You tasted it earlier. You need to take another sip now."

The rice wine tasted bitter, pungent, like cough medicine laced with pepper powder. I just took a small sip. The liquid burned as it went down my throat. My eyes began to swell and my sight became blurred. I wasn't turning blue, was I? I reached out my hands and put them under the table lamp. They looked normal. I took another, bigger sip of wine and soon my whole body felt like it was on fire. I lifted up my clothes and my tummy looked very pale in the lamp light. There was no sign of blue.

"Am I turning blue?" I asked Dad.

"No, Chen Miaomiao," he said.

But why did Mom turn blue? How could that blue mass be my Mom? A genuine sorrow began to overwhelm me. Mom used to be such a funny person who often talked about some meaningless things. Her fingers were always cold. But she was such a gentle person. In winter, before her hands would touch my body, she would try to warm them first. But where was she now? She had been turned into something alien and frightening to me.

I began to cry.

"Don't cry, don't cry," Dad said, holding me in his arms. "That's why your mother never throws a shadow in photos. The camera tells the truth. Mom is just like a paper-thin cloud that hardly registers on film."

He told me Mom would be back to her old self in the morning and I could ask her all the questions I wanted.

"Does that mean you have seen her like this before?" I asked.

Dad nodded. "When your Mom was about to give birth to you, she refused to go to the hospital because they use ethanol there and that's a form of alcohol."

To think that Dad and Mom had hidden this from me for so many years! I couldn't collect my thoughts. I didn't know what to think.

"Are you afraid?" I asked Dad.

"Yes," he replied. "But I have no way out."

"What are you afraid of?" I asked, pressing the question harder because I still had the feeling he was concealing something from me.

Dad said that he was afraid that he would end up like Xu Xian. [Xu Xian is the hero in a famous Chinese legend who had a romance with a white snake fairy and the couple experienced many hardships – Translator]

Ah! Suddenly it all became clearer. Mom was just like the white snake fairy, who always shied away from alcohol. Once touched by alcohol, it would show its original shape. So, things said in fairy tales could happen in real life. Was Mom as kind and capable as the White Snake? Could she become invisible? Could she fly? Could she conjure things she wanted out from the air?

I wanted to take a leak and asked Dad to accompany me to the bathroom. I was a big girl now, so Dad turned his head away to avoid the embarrassment of looking at me while I was peeing. But I made such a loud, spurting sound that I felt embarrassed. Still, I didn't dare stay in the bathroom alone. Mom's red toothbrush mug stared at me like a big Mexican bird perched in front of the mirror. Mom's pink towel was hanging on the rack, and I swore it gave itself a little shake. Looking at what used to be just ordinary things, I first felt an aching in my heart and I began to shiver. Suddenly, all Mom's things seemed to have a spirit in them.

Dad said: "Don't be scared. You are my child and I will protect you."

Actually, I wasn't feeling scared anymore. I was feeling agitated. Across the sitting room and down the corridor, I could see Mom in her bed. She was still blue. Her face was blurry. She was lying quietly underneath the printed cloth quilt. Was this really the woman who had always been so understanding and kind-hearted with me?

I saw her hand move a little. It reminded my of the times she touched my body and I felt a warmness in my heart. Just then, a finger from Mom's hand shook and a tiny blinking blue blob began to fly towards me like a small moth. It stopped in front of me. It was an embroidered blue flower from a French clothing label that Mom particularly liked.

I opened my hands and the little flower landed on my palm. It was wet and cold, like ice.

I let out another scream and threw off the flower from my hand.

Dad, who by this time had had more to drink than usual and was slumped in a chair, jumped to his feet as the little blue flower dropped to the carpet and melted into a splotch of water.

That night, Dad sat at my bedside as I went to sleep. At midnight, I heard the sound of someone opening the door of our little storeroom. Since it wasn't used too often, the door squeaked loudly. I raised my head and saw Dad still sitting on the edge of my bed, with his head slumped in deep sleep. If Mom came to eat me, I thought, she would have to remove Dad first, and that wouldn't be an easy job. He reeked of wine.

Before I fell asleep again, I scolded myself for being so selfish. In ancient times, a child would offer himself as a sacrifice to a tiger in order to save his father. But see what I had done! The shame was on me.

Chapter II

Feeling Is
the Stickiest Glue

When I woke up, the whole room was already flooded with sunshine. I could hear cars running along Nanjing Road W. outside there and the policeman standing in the middle of the road blowing his whistle.

Mom was sitting on the floor, looking at me. She looked again like ever before. A little thinner though, her eyebrows were quite light and there was a red beauty spot. She was wearing a large white tee shirt embroidered with a little, light bluish flower. The same hue as Mom had been last night.

I grasped my quilt up around me and shouted out: "Quick, Dad, come here!"

Dad was still asleep, no doubt reeling from the effects of too much drink the night before.

"Don't be afraid of me," Mom said. "I'll never hurt anyone."

She clapped her hands, then showed them to me. There was nothing in her hands and even her fingernails all looked quite normal.

I was still skeptical. Even a wolf knew how to disguise itself as an amiable granny.

She stuck out her tongue to show me. There was no fresh blood on it.

Mom said, "What can I say so that you will believe me?"

She thought a moment and then said, "Our bodies are cold, somewhat like the ice cream but not sweet. Meanwhile, human bodies are warm, particularly when they have drunk wine. The wine kindles fire in their bodies. So, when we touch human beings, it's like putting ice cream under the sun. You see, it is we who are afraid of human beings, not the other way around. You really don't have anything to be afraid of from me."

Mom was another kind of being, just as Dad said. She told me blue humans could fly, and lived in another space, with fairies and mermaids. Her kin were more fragile than our human form, making them susceptible to being blown away by a mere zephyr of air. While we humans could not enter the realm where they lived, they could enter our world but only at specific time in a day. They could walk and they could fly. In a way, they were superior to us.

"It this all true?" I asked her.

"It is," Mom said. "You are my child. Why should I lie to you? You can look into my eyes and see it is true."

Mom leaned toward me. Her brown eyes were soft and honest.

"My child, never should you be afraid of me," she said. "I can do a lot of things for you that other moms cannot do for their children."

"Like what?" I asked.

She stretched out a hand and grasped at the air. Then, finger by finger, she opened her hand. In her palm was an electronic chicken that Dad has refused to buy for me despite my repeated begging.

"How about this?" said Mom, with a slightly smug expression on her face.

She handed me the toy, then got up to fetch a banknote from a drawer. She folded it into an origami crane, put it on her palm and blew at it. "Abracadabra, abracadabra. Fly to the white and blue department store on Huaihai Road," she chanted softly. Then she opened a window and floated the crane into the air outside.

Mom turned to me and said, "We can't take anything from a store without paying. That would be stealing. I won't do bad things just because others can't see it."

I held the toy chicken in my hands. In "Aladdin and the Wonderful Lamp," the hero was helped by a genie, and in "Pinocchio," the puppet was befriended by a fairy. How I had always admired those tales of magic. I had never expected to discover one day that my Mom lived in such a fairy tale realm.

Mom sat there and suddenly she started to laugh without uttering a sound. Her whole face was laughing, her eyes shone, her face glowed and her eyebrows were raised like two birds flying in opposite directions. She blinked at me, as though amused by my thoughts, which she must have been able to read.

Suddenly, Mom put a hand to her eye and a blue flower appeared where her eyeball had been. The eyeball was now in her hand. She kneaded it to soften it and produced another small blue flower. In the middle of the flower I saw a blinking eye. Mom said, "Abracadabra, abracadabra, go to the primary school near Jing'an Temple."

And with those words, the flower flew away.

Then Mom said to me, "I see a large room, where someone is cutting up a frog with many children looking on. Blood is oozing from the frog. It's unbelievable that anyone can treat a frog like that."

I said, "It's not us. It's the biology teacher. In the future, there will be thousands of frog souls haunting him. I hate killing frogs." Mom knew my favorite animal was the frog.

She withdrew into silence for a few minutes before talking to me again. "Your friend Li Yuchen is doing her English homework," she said. "My heavens, she's biting her pencil!"

"That's because she hates the homework," I said.

Li Yuchen was my best friend. She lived nearby so we always went to school together and we both sat in the fourth row of the classroom. She was a small, skinny girl, and her eyes always blinked fast, just like a little rabbit. Although I didn't consider her my soulmate, I still liked her. She was a good student, but, like me, she loathed homework.

"Then she must be a gifted child," my mother said. "Under the pressure of homework, her talent is being squeezed out through her teeth. That's why she bites pencils."

Her parents were divorced and she lived with her father. She was a bit like a homeless kid, which was perhaps why I was drawn to her. I had tried to be friends with the best students in the class, but so many of them were selfish and condescending. So I had turned to the underdogs to find friendship. Li Yuchen was one of them and she had proven to be a loyal friend. Though I didn't escape the periodic feeling that I was doing all the giving.

"Kids with divorced parents are all like that," I said.

"What if your father and I got a divorce?" Mom asked. Her remaining eyeball scrutinized me.

"You won't, will you?" I asked.

" But what if we did?" Mom persisted.

"I don't know," I replied, unhappy with the turn of the conversation. "Don't say those kinds of things."

Mom sighed and said, "Your Teacher Wang has scalded her foot while preparing hot milk for your classmates. She's hopping around on one foot."

Then I realized that Mom's other eyeball had been transported to our classroom. I shook my head in disbelief.

"Could you have a look in the boys' toilet?" I asked.

Mom was startled. "Why do that?" she asked.

"Nothing, just curious," I said. "I am just curious what boys look like."

Mom shook her head and said, "Chen Miaomiao, you have a dirty mind."

I could not help but laugh. I knew every corner of our school except the boys' toilets and wondered what they look like inside.

"They have white tiles and short wooden doors," she said, reading my mind.

"Hmmm, almost the same in the girls," I thought.

Then Mom turned more serious. "I cannot tell you how boys look when they stand up and pee. Once girls learn those things, they stop growing. You are already too short."

Mom winked and the flower on her eye turned back into an eyeball.

Wow, Mom was fabulous! She was better than the fairy in "Pinocchio" and the genie in "Aladdin". I knew now that she wasn't a monster who would eat me. She would always be on my side.

Mom looked at me, all smiles. She used to have a slight sadness in her face, like a glass pane that hadn't been cleaned for some time. But now her face was clear and glowing as I had never seen it before.

In her joyful face there was beauty.

"Can you also fly?" I asked.

Mom blinked once and then slowly levitated. She floated across the room. She had taken flight without any sudden movement. Not like little birds who flapped their wings hard before they took off. Mom touched the ceiling, all the while smiling down at me.

"Dad!" I shouted out, but Mom quickly hushed me.

She floated over where Dad was still fast asleep. Looking closely at his face, she grimaced. She would never do that if Dad were awake. But he continued in his deep sleep, unaware of what was going on.

I laughed at the scene.

Then Mom kissed Dad on his face and began to mimic Dad, closing her eyes as though intoxicated. She would never have dared to do that had he been awake. I burst into a fit of laughter.

Dad stirred, and Mom, startled, floated higher like a wisp of smoke.

She pointed at the bulb in the overhead light. "My goodness," she said, "it's so dirty. I must clean that today."

"That doesn't sound very exciting," I said.

Mom was all smiles.

"Chen Miaomiao," she stifled a giggle and said, "you are lazy. Someday the home you live in will be messy."

Mom was floating about the room, finding a cobweb above the curtains and dust in the picture rails on the wall.

"Mom, can I fly with you?" I asked.

She approached me from above and grasped me by the hand. Her touch was warm. Then she cuddled me in my bed. She smelled somewhat like a freshly cut cucumber. I felt warm inside.

My bed seemed to be becoming smaller and narrower. Suddenly I found myself looking at things stored on the top of the wardrobe. There, amid some dust, were some paintings Mom had abandoned when half done but loathed to throw away.

My head hit something hard. I looked up and found myself staring at the ceiling. I was flying!!!

Mom and I hovered along the ceiling as we floated about the house. We were like two birds. Accidentally, we bumped into the ceiling light. "Oh, don't let it drop!" Mom cried out.

Peeking out the louver window, I could see the intersection of Nanjing Road and Shaanxi Road below. The whistle-blowing young policeman stood with a straight back on the round podium in the middle of the intersection, directing traffic. What would he think if he saw a girl flying? Would he remember that he had yelled at me a few days ago when I started to dash across the street, then stopped traffic to usher me across?

"I want to fly outside," I said.

"No," Mom said, "We can't do that. People will see us."

"But, Mom," I implored her.

"No," she said firmly. "Really we can't do that. In the world of man, we must behave like man. We can't let others know that we are different. We vowed that before we came here. Otherwise, we would not have been allowed to come."

In saying that, I was gently lowered to the floor. Mom came down, too.

"I love you, Chen Miaomiao," she said. "And when we love, there is a sticky glue that oozes from our hearts. It binds into feelings."

In her realm, she told me, people never showed emotion because they didn't have feelings. Their hearts were made of light crystals. They never got angry or expressed joy. They never fought or loved. They didn't even talk and had no language. Light as air, they floated about, with the wind as their music.

Her people came to our world in search of feelings. Mom said she wanted to glue herself to Dad and me.

"I waited for many days to come here," she said. "After a group of us arrived, we hid in an unoccupied old church of red bricks. It was very quiet there. The angels in the church were also of our kind. We had to stay there a while to get used to the strong heat of this world. Most of us lost weight.

"We came out at dusk because we were afraid of the sunshine," she said. "We flew into the big tree outside and played there. We held onto leaves, swinging and singing. People under the tree could not hear us singing and could not see us either. They thought it was the rustling of the leaves. Those were people who would not have any paths crossing with ours.

"Those who did look up trying to find something beyond the leaves were either poets or lost souls looking for love. They could hear the faint sounds of song."

"From the tree, we looked down at the faces below us, deciding who was the most handsome. That was the precondition for us to fall in love with a human. We tended to love puzzled faces because puzzlement is also a form of feeling. If it whizzed toward our hearts like an arrow, then a sticky substance would ooze from my heart, and bit by bit, a feeling would be stuck together.

"I fell in love with your Dad just like that," she said. "Your father was a university student. Every Saturday after school, he waited for the bus home under that tree. He was attending the First Medical Institute, but also wrote poetry. His eyes looking upward were the stickiest thing in the world."

As she spoke, a red light crossed her face, just as the blue had done the day before.

It was the first time I had ever heard how my parents had met. I felt proud to be their child.

Mom said her heart became stickier when I was born. Her words reminded me of the princess mermaid in H.C. Anderson's fairy tale. The little mermaid wanted to be a human being. Mom told me once she dived into the depths of the sea and saw princess mermaid there. But she was an unhappy mermaid because no human had fallen in love with her.

"Where's that tree?" I asked.

"At the terminus of Bus Route 49, in front of the church. I will take you to see it someday," Mom said. "It's the gravestone of your parents' love."

"Stop talking nonsense," I replied, imitating my father's tone. I realized now why she often had difficulty expressing herself with the right words.

Then, I heard movement behind us. Dad was standing at the door. At the sight of him, Mom's smile vanished.

Chapter III
A Kid's Life Is Not Easy

Standing at the door, Dad looked at us for a quite long while and then said he wanted to divorce Mom.

I was stunned. There had been no quarrels, no fighting. It wasn't a question of another woman in his life. There had been no disharmony in the household. I didn't understand and I stared at my father in complete disbelief.

Sensing my shock, my father took a gentler tone. He said he and Mom had agreed on the day I was born that they would divorce once I learned the truth about Mom. Though alienated from one another for years, they had endeavored to cover it up. He said they wanted me to grow up as a normal, happy child.

I was too stunned to speak. Suddenly nothing in my life seemed real. It had never been real. I pinched myself hard and it hurt badly. I was not dreaming.

Dad gazed at me sadly and said no more. Mom leaned against the door frame, also silent. She just looked at me and Dad, her eyes as wide and engaging as those of a teddy bear in a store, hoping someone would come to buy it.

We used to be a family. Now all was lost. How could life continue here?

At that moment, the phone rang. It was Teacher Wang, inquiring about my absence from school.

Dad stuttered as he tried to lie about the situation. Teacher Wang apparently didn't want to hear what he was saying. Her voice came loudly out of the phone. She said I couldn't afford to miss classes, in a scolding tone. I had no outside tutor, and although I was a smart child, my grades weren't up to par. After the junior middle school entrance exams were cancelled, the school had set up a cram class for students who had good grades and wanted to qualify for the accelerated curriculum. Once you got into that class, you had one foot in the best of high schools. Other parents were trying their very best in order to squeeze their children into that class. And now here I was, daring to be truant.

"Is your family out of its mind?" Teacher Wang thundered over the phone. "What can possibly be more important than Chen Miaomiao's examination? I just can't figure it out!"

Dad reverted to sweet talk and promised her that I would be back in school. Then he hung up.

"Your teacher is right," he said with a sigh. "Nothing is more important than studies. So eat something now and go back to school. Teacher Wang complained that every morning, you talk about 'Growing Pains' in class, so starting today, you won't be allowed to watch TV until the cram class enrollment ends."

I was still speechless.

"Everything else can wait," he said. "At this moment, you are still the top priority."

Mom sighed with relief and dashed into the kitchen to prepare lunch. Then, I could tell that the divorce was Dad's idea, not hers.

I also felt a big relief. School would be a nice diversion from the dramas of the last day.

Our school operated under a nine-year system. In order to offer more courses to fifth-graders with good grades and better prepare them for senior middle school entrance exams, the school had set up an elite class. Parents quickly took the class seriously, striving to get their children enrolled.

At a parent-teacher meeting, Teacher Wang told my Mom and Dad that many other parents had hired family tutors for their children. People always said: "To grind one's spear just before the battle may not sharpen it much but it can at least make it shine." Tutors had been selected from teachers at the No. 1 Middle School, where our new schoolmaster had been transferred from. Teachers from that esteemed school would know best how to prepare students for the elite class selection test. Teacher Wang suggested that all parents who could afford it should consider getting a tutor.

Since then Dad had been trying to find the best tutor for me but had not been happy with the choices.

Dad was the kind of person who read people by their faces. Not able to find a tutor, he had dismissed the need for one. I tended to agree with him. I had grown weary of school, all the endless homework. In the back of my mind, I had resigned myself to not doing well on the test.

Most students, who had tutors and were preparing feverishly for the test, had stopped all after-school recreation. They drank the Brands, a traditional essence of chicken, because their parents believed it would help nourish their brains. Every teacher told us one hundred times a day: "Make best use of your time and work for that last sprint to the finish. How many opportunities do you think one has in life?" The words echoed through my mind, scaring me.

Those who failed the test and could not attend a good senior middle school would have little chance of entering a good university. Without education in a good university, one could hardly find a good job, which in return would mean a poor life and hardships. I didn't want to lead a life of pain, so I had resolved to study harder.

But tried as I might, I didn't get good grade. My teachers said I was the kind of student who could attain high goals if I were just motivated. I needed to apply myself more. But as my grades kept coming up short, I despaired.

I was afraid of exams. Dad could see that. "When I sat for the college entrance examinations, I aced all other science major students at our school," he said. "I see the next generation isn't made of the same stuff."

"Ah," I replied, "I wish you could transform yourself back into a child and sit the exams for me."

Mom tried to be supportive. When I toiled over homework, she always patted me on the back and said: "Alas, you are still such a child."

The countdown was on. A small blackboard appeared at school, advising us how many days were left before the exams. Every day the number ticked lower. I couldn't stand the sight of the blackboard. It gave me a stomach ache. No one liked it, not even Teacher Wang. "Whenever I see it, my heart skip a beat for you," she told our class. "Are you all ready for it or not?"

Teacher Wang was always nice to us in the morning. At ten, we all drank milk after she had put all the little cartons in a red plastic bucket of hot water to warm it up.

However, by afternoon, as the workload piled on, we were all dog tired and lost our concentration. We turned unruly, causing Teacher Wang to intervene with a stern hand.

Standing on the dais, she singled out one of us for a tongue-lashing, which was meant to reprimand all of us. By the time the day ended, she would sigh and say, "I'm going to die in your hands."

After a lunch with no further mention of divorce, Dad walked me to school, using the opportunity to stress the importance of the exam, as if my whole life hung on it.

When we arrived at school, I went into class and Dad went to Teacher Wang's office to ask for morning leave for me in arrears. I could tell by his face that it was an unpleasant undertaking for him because Teacher Wang's sternness could be formidable.

Most of my classmates used the noon break to do homework. Heavenly King, the black sheep in our class, was once again ordered by a teacher to stand in front of the blackboard as a penalty for talking in class without permission. The class monitor was jotting down names of students to be reported for breaking this rule or that. The monitor used to be a friend of mine, but no longer because she was bossy and treated me like her lackey.

Li Yuchen's and my desks were separated by a narrow aisle. She raised her head from the exercise book as I came in. Her face was yellowish, with a bulging blue vein crawling along the bridge of her nose. "You are in trouble," she said. "We have 13 exercise books to work on today and you didn't do anything this morning. You are not going to get any sleep tonight."

Sitting at my desk and looking about the familiar trappings of the classroom, I felt strange. Since yesterday, I had undergone a change while here, nothing had changed. I felt as I had returned from a distant place.

I glanced repeatedly at Li Yuchen. "Do you want borrow an eraser?" she asked, perplexed by the expression on my face. In fact, I wanted to talk to someone about all the things that had happened at home, but I couldn't find the words. Though Li Yuchen and I usually walked home from school together, we weren't in the habit of baring our souls.

No one knew what earth-shattering things had happened to me, even my best friend. She was still looking at me, waiting for an answer. "I just wanted to ask if you have a tutor yet," I finally said.

"My Dad didn't say he's going to find one for me," she said. "He's so busy and hardly stays at home. In the past five evenings, I had all my suppers at the Yonghe Soybean Milk Eatery."

Yes, it was tough living in a divorced family.

Teacher Wang appeared in the doorway. "I just gave your father a good lecture," she said, pointing at me.

It was raining when school let out. Li Yuchen shared my umbrella on the way home. Without a mother to remind her, she always forgot to carry an umbrella to school. My desk-mate grabbed her umbrella and followed us. She always barged in where she wasn't wanted. She always wanted to be the center of attention and was pushy about it. Li Yuchen and I had only a short bit of free time together every day and we didn't want it wasted by her presence.

We purposely walked fast, but she kept pace. "Let's play the tracker's game," she told us. "Wherever you go, I will follow."

Li Yuchen and I ignored her. We came to the stop for Tram Route 20, where my desk-mate usually got on. But this day she kept following along with us.

"That's your tram stop," I said.

"I am taking the tram at the next stop because that's what my mother told me to do," she said.

I suspected she was lying.

Finally, at the next tram stop, we got rid of her. We turned the corner onto Taixing Road.

My home was nearer, but I decided I would walk Li Yuchen to her door. She knew that my Mom worked at home and was always there to greet me at the door. "You are a lucky girl," she said.

I asked Li Yuchen what it was like to go home to an empty house. "You get used to it," she said, with a shrug.

Li Yuchen's apartment building stood in front of a large empty lot, where houses had been demolished to make way for a new shopping mall. The lot had sat empty for such a long time that weeds and grasses were overrunning it. I told Li Yuchen that the sight of such a forlorn space gave me the creeps.

"I feel the same," she said. "Our bathroom window looks out over the lot. At night, especially when the moon is out, I don't dare go to the bathroom. It's very weird and scary."

We arrived at her apartment block and Li Yuchen disappeared inside. I suddenly felt lonely. On the way home, I saw a girl selling hot green onion pancakes at the street corner. Her red coat was soaked from the rain.

Mom sometimes met me at the school gate when class was dismissed. She said I was too thin and my book satchel too heavy for me to carry. She kept her arm around me all the way home. If Li Yuchen was with us, Mom always offered to carry her bag, too, but Li Yuchen always declined until my mother pressed her to relent.

If we walked around that corner and the girl in red coat was still there, Mom would stop and buy three green onion pancakes for the three of us to munch on the way home. Mom always said the green onion pancakes were for the nose, not the stomach. Even after eating the pancakes, the aroma followed us deliciously home.

Chapter IV
There Are Ways to Beat Exams

Daunted by his encounter with Teacher Wang, Dad found a student at the Jiao Tong University, who was a graduate from the No. 1 Middle School, to be my tutor. He said any student who had managed to get into such a good university would know how to teach me to take the exams.

The student wore glasses. His face was pimpled and his nose jutted forward like a bird's beak. I liked him immediately.

First off, he told me that the exams were not the most important thing in life. If a child lived only to take exams and enter university, he would be bored and die. Dad, who was nearby, was clearly irritated. "That's nonsense talk," he finally said, and told my new tutor

47

that his services would no longer be needed. On his way out, the student held the door and stared directly at Dad. Feeling uneasy, Dad looked down and said: "I'm sorry. In my heart, I understand what you said. I was university student. I understand."

The student summoned up his courage and said, "No, you don't understand. In your generation, all students wanted to get into university but couldn't. So, you have gone mad with the idea of education. People like you have ruined the life of our generation and you now want to ruin the life of your little girl."

Mom dashed forward and stood in front of Dad.

"Everyone is mad," she said. "Everyone wants to be the same as everyone else. Even if you have to pretend, you must act like the others. You don't understand. Everyone wants what he doesn't have. No one intends to harm others. When you talked to our Chen Miaomiao, you had the same motivation."

After the student left, Dad sat in his old rocking chair without saying a word.

Mom went to sit next to him and said, "Did you see the big chin on that student? How could he utter anything gentle?"

"Actually he was right," Dad replied. "Under the current education system, only someone who has already entered a famous university could make such remarks. The losers in the competition don't even have the luxury to talk about psychological crisis."

Mom asked: "What do you think then?"

"We still have to find a tutor for Chen Miaomiao," he said. "She is not an outstanding student. Even those students who are nearly hundred percent sure they can pass the exam have already employed tutors, so how can we not?"

"I'll take care of it," Mom said.

"But you have never even attended school," he said, giving Mom an irritated look.

Mom flashed a smile. She used one of her hands to gently dig into one eye, taking out the eyeball. After kneading and pulling it, the eyeball was turned into blue toy clay. She pressed it several times and made it into a little blue flower with an eye as its heart. Mom put the flower in her hand and then threw it skyward. The flower stuck to the ceiling, and in the place of Mom's eyeball, a little blue flower blossomed.

Dad sat watching, dumfounded.

"I will find whoever has hired the best family tutor and begin a live TV broadcast," she said.

Dad said he was hesitant about such trickery, though I sat there elated. But Dad was like that. He disliked anything that was not black and white.

"This is only taking a little bit of advantage of something," my mother said. "You see, the tutor won't know there is an extra student listening to him, quiet as a mouse, without disturbing anyone."

After considering her words for a few seconds, Dad nodded. "So, this means we can benefit at no expense to anyone else," he said, conceding that a bit of flexibility might be wise.

Mom, grateful for his acquiescence, went over to touch him, but he deflected her hand.

Then she pointed a finger in the air and the little blue flower fell back into her hands. She asked: "Now where should we find the best tutor?"

Dad opened a notebook full of names and addresses of teachers from No. 1 Middle School. His finger moved down the list, stopping at Teacher Liu. I recalled hearing that Teacher Liu was the best instructor of Chinese, which was one of my hardest courses.

Actually, I had liked Chinese when I first began learning to write compositions. I wrote things I could never talk to people about, but later I found that my thoughts contradicted those of my teacher. I ended up with poor grades, and Teacher Liu impatiently told me I just didn't have the hang of it. I wasn't emphasizing the ideas she wanted. As time passed, I came to hate composition.

Mom plucked one of her ears and turned it into another flower. "The eye will go to see and the ear will listen."

I hurried to open the window and Mom flipped the flowers out. After a few minutes, Mom said: "Teacher Liu is really busy. There are four students taking lessons in her home. She's talking about composition and asking the students to go back and work on a composition with the title 'My xx.' It's a typical profile composition."

"Maybe we should follow a student who has just started to take the cram lessons," Dad said. "Otherwise it won't help because we have missed all the classes before."

Mom said, "That's okay. We'll wait for the next boy. He and his father are now waiting in the living room."

Dad said: "Fine, let's follow him." Then he gave me a push and said: "Quick, go and get your school bag and get ready for the lesson."

That night, Dad, Mom and me sat at the table. One of Mom's eyes was covered by a blue flower. She loudly repeated every word said by Teacher Liu. I was used to look into the face of the one whom I was listening to. Watching Mom's face with a little blue flower, I admired how beautiful she was. Mom imitated Teacher Liu's voice. I could immediately tell that she was a teacher. Her voice rose and fell with accentuations at some key points, just like singing. It's not easy for Mom to mimic Teacher Liu so vividly.

Teacher Liu's first lesson focused on how to highlight the key parts of a composition. The lead should be made up of no more than four sentences. They must be brief and directly introduce the hero. Then, one could write an episode or a positive example to illustrate him.

That could be followed by a negative example. One or two other episodes could be used to describe the hero from sidelines. These would be the second part of the composition, which would take about 300 characters. More verbs and more descriptions could be employed to paint the characteristics. The third part would be the ending, which should also be kept brief.

Actually, this was the least exciting, just like filling in blanks. But now, I couldn't care too much whether it's exciting or not. I tried damn hard to writing down all the golden rules of Teacher Liu and I could deal with the rest later on. Following Teacher Liu's formula, writing a composition was just a piece of cake, no need for brains.

Sitting opposite me, Dad was stunned by Teacher Liu's lesson. It was not until the class was over, homework assigned and Mom retrieved her eye and ear and put them back onto her face did Dad open his mouth: "How could anyone write a composition like this? It's purely for exams. You can never learn anything about how to express yourself. In this way, kids will definitely be deprived of all their inspirations."

Dad shook his head so vigorously that his hair fell to cover his eyes. He said: "Isn't it destroying the kids?"

I immediately talked back: "Does it dawn on you just now?"

Mom said: "Let's follow Teacher Liu's way to pass the exam first."

Next day, Mom and Dad repeated the ritual in finding a math teacher for me. His home was more crowded than Teacher Liu's and the new boy who appeared there turned out to be Heavenly King. His mom told Teacher Wang that they didn't have much hope in the kid. But behind people's backs, they looked for a tutor for him. They wanted to turn Teacher Wang's headache into a black horse, so all teachers wouldn't look down upon naughty kids any more.

Heavenly King was assigned to the 6-7pm session on Sunday. The teacher agreed to take the boy because of his father's endless pleading. His father said he was willing to double the fee payment.

At beginning, the teacher was a bit displeased. He said: "That's my meal time." In other words, he meant that one had to eat, right. "It will be followed by other students, who are scheduled to be here by 7:30."

Heavenly King's father said: "Teacher, there has never been a college student in our family. We are just ordinary people, with little connections. It took us great efforts to find your address. Now, times are different and it should be our turn to enjoy some sunshine and let our kid find a good job. The kid is all the hope of our family. So, I beg you to take him."

Hearing a man make such passionate remarks, the teacher was taken aback for a moment and then he said: "All right."

I followed Heavenly King in the math lesson.

Mom said the boy's father really didn't seem to be well-off. His shoes would cost only 50 yuan during sales.

Dad said: "The whole society is mad now, as all parents expect their kids to excel."

I immediately said: "You are no exception."

Quite upset, Dad said: "Don't you sass. Instinctively, I don't want you to win any fame. I only hope you can be a happy person. Now, I am forced by the ethos among all other parents to do what I'm doing. I am forced by others to do things against my original intention. More precisely, it's you kiddo who has forced me to give up my principles."

I was so mad that I began to laugh: "I force you what? I myself have been very much peeved." Dad just talked mumble jumble. Probably, this was because his work required only deft hands not sharp tongues.

Dad said: "You force me to do things that, I know clearly, are wrong. So do your school and teachers."

Finally, it was Mom who pulled me away. She said: "Stop piquing your father, he's just worrying that you might not do well in the test."

I said: "Ok, it's for you that I'll stop picking a bone with him." In fact, I just talked tough. In my inner heart, I was also afraid that Dad would get really mad and hit me. In the fight between a kid and an adult, there had never been any justice to talk about. Whoever was bigger would be the winner. To win a battle with an adult, I got to wait for the day when I was grown up.

Despite his complaining, Dad did just what he had complained about. He bought home a large blackboard and many chalks. He propped up the blackboard in the living room and asked Mom to write down all that the tutors wrote to their students. Mom acted like a teacher. I sensed Mom liked this a lot, which made her believe that she was very capable.

It was simply inhumane to go through the preparations for the exam day and night. I did often wake up in midnight and then could not fall asleep again for a long time. Before when my desk neighbor told me that she frequently suffered from insomnia, I thought she was talking nonsense and she just wanted to say that she's different. Now, I started to believe her. In the middle of the night, I often heard noise of the door of our storeroom. The door squeaked as if someone open the door and get into the storeroom, where we only stored some boxes and dried food. I didn't believe anyone would go to there to get some dried white fungus and cook it in the dead of night. I thought it must be some illusion.

After I took lessons from two tutors, I began to gain better and better marks in class tests and mock exams. Teacher Wang often took me as a good example when she criticized other students who back paddled. At the same time, she also asked me how would I make such fast progresses. What could I say? I explained that my Mom and Dad helped me with my homework everyday on rotation. So, Teacher Wang also praised my Mom and Dad in the class. When I told Mom about this, she was so happy as if she wanted to turn herself into a child next time so she would go to school everyday. Although Mom was a fairy, she had the same shortcomings as human beings. Hearing others praise her, she couldn't help but burst into laughter, revealing her big teeth.

So many tidy, white, big teeth!

I had found out that even Mom didn't drink wine and didn't turn blue, I could still find something in her which indicated that she's different from real human. For one thing, I had never seen anyone got white teeth like Mom's. Once, I was in the room of the granny of one of my classmates and I saw some white teeth like Mom's dipped in the water in a green porcelain bowl. But that were the granny's false teeth. Only false things would be perfect like that.

After Teacher Wang praised me in the class, Li Yuchen said to me: "Your mom's really cool. She could tutor you on both Chinese and math. Sometimes, I also asked my father to help me on math, but even he didn't know how to do it though he's a college graduate. He said what he learned is different from what I'm learning now."

I almost wanted to tell Li Yuchen the truth, but I couldn't. I also wanted very much to help her and invited her to my home to listen to Mom's talking. But I couldn't do that either. Sometimes, the words were already on the tip of my tongue before I swallowed them down. I felt like I ate a tea-flavored egg, which choked in the middle of my throat.

Li Yuchen never asked to come to my home. Anything I didn't say, she never asked. I had learned this trait from her. So, I tried not to ask any questions that might make her feel difficult. Mom said Li Yuchen was a very intelligent child, overly mature and pitiful.

During every tutorial lesson, I took copious notes and passed them on to Li Yuchen next day. So, she could review the lessons by following my notes. Later I found that doing this actually helped me to better memorize the lessons. Maybe, this was what people said good deeds would always be rewarded.

I could very well understand the sparkles in the big eyes of Li Yuchen. My Mom had reminded her of her own mother. Sometimes after the refreshing lessons, she would suddenly ask me in whisper: "Does you mother make any gurgling sound when she drinks water? My mom did and so loud, just like a cow."

At such moment, I felt sharing an empathy with Li Yuchen. How I wanted to talk a little more about my Mom. For me, it's so hard to keep a secret. I really wished someone would come to discuss this kind of things with me. I was scared in my heart. My Mom was so different. This thing was utterly unbelievable to begin with, and I didn't think it would last forever. I often got a feeling that Mom would vanish very quickly. I didn't want to talk to Mom and Dad about this feeling and pretended that I was not feeling anything special. I just kept the fear inside myself.

Going on like this, gradually the number on the small blackboard was down to "2". Only two days left before we sat in the exam for re-assigning classes. It was Thursday. After such a long time of preparation, the moment of revelation was approaching. Finally,

Teacher Wang told us: "Starting from now on, don't stay up late at night and don't watch television. Just relax, relax and take a good rest. In this way, your brain may work better. It's already too late to make the last minute prayer to the Buddha."

I didn't know why, but the moment the teacher left the classroom, all of us let loose a scream in unison just like a kind of hurrah. Everyone was laughing with wide-opened eyes. Heavenly King was the first to leave his seat. He stomped the floor and yelled: "Zero points, 100 points, zero points, 100 points!"

Girls were all sitting on their desks, giggling.

One student took the cap off his head and threw it towards the ceiling. Immediately, everyone was throwing anything they could lay hands on towards the ceiling. Handkerchiefs, lunch box bags and even shoes. Heavenly King's shoes must be the most fetid in the world and they were big, too. He must be crazy now and he also took off his shoes and threw them around. One happened to fall on the shoulder of my neighbor. She was frozen for a minute. We all thought she would begin to cry, but instead she let out a big laughter.

In one corner, a bevy of girls began to sing noisily: "Twist your heads, shake your asses, let's do some exercises." And they were all wagging their asses violently.

Everyone was mad. I didn't understand what to celebrate about today.

Finally, Teacher Wang's face popped up in the door frame. She was so stunned by the scene that her eyebrows almost dropped. She said: "Are you all going out of your mind?"

Then, she hurried all us home. She said: "This is just the beginning. Don't you think that's all the life has in stock for you. In the future, there will be numerous, more crucial exams in the pipeline." She escorted us across the street as if we were still first-graders. She stood in the middle of the road and stretched out her arms to block a car, like a hen protecting her chicken. She did not leave until all of us crossed the street. She was concerned about us, but she didn't want us to know it.

At the moment to part with Li Yuchen, she suddenly felt sad: "I think I'm not going to make it. Anyway, no one in my family cares about it. Other kids study for their parents, who see their marks as more important than their own lives. I just don't know for whom I have been studying for."

Recently, she had decided to keep long hair, but she didn't really know how to do it. So, her hair hanged down unkempt, making her little chin face look as sharp as the tip of scissors.

Then, an idea suddenly flashed across my mind.

A shocking idea.

I said to Li Yuchen: "What would you do at home today?"

She shook her head.

I said: "You must wait for my phone. I'll call you home."

"Why?" she asked.

"My Mom will help me for the final review of all the lessons and I will tell you about it."

Li Yuchen gave me a pat.

Chapter V
A Fairy Flies to the Human World

Getting home, Mom opened the door for me. Seeing the dull look on my face, she immediately became concerned. She asked, "What's wrong with you? What's wrong?"

"Nothing," I said, pushing her away.

I handed her my school bag and went directly into the bathroom. I sat on the edge of the bathtub and waited. Mom became more agitated. She began to knock on the door. Inside the bathroom it was quiet except for the sound of water dripping from the tap. But I didn't pay much attention to that or anything. I was preoccupied with thoughts of the exam. Mom and Dad had begun to pity me. Had I worked hard enough? What if I screwed up the exam?

Originally, I just wanted to put on a show for Mom. Now, thinking about it, I began to panic.

"Miao, what happened?" Mom asked from the other side of the door in a loud voice. "Do you have a stomach ache or some other ailment?"

Crestfallen, I opened the door and walked over to a chair to sit down. Mom came to my side and hugged me. "The exam isn't everything," she said. "There's nothing to be scared of."

I looked into her eyes. I wouldn't be afraid any more if a flower bloomed in one of her eyes and she again murmured "abracadabra, abracadabra." How much I wished I were a fairy, too.

"You don't understand," I said. "It's really scary. This afternoon, the whole class went mad."

I told her about Li Yuchen and Mom felt so sad that tears welled in her eyes. One big teardrop fell from her face to the table and splashed into five smaller water spots, like a tiny flower.

"I wish I could help you two," Mom said.

My heartbeat suddenly began to accelerate.

"You could help me," I said, my eyes brightening.

"How?" she asked.

"I won't tell you because you will just say no," I said.

"I must first know what you are talking about before I can say yes or no." she said.

My heart began to pound more wildly in my chest. Then I said: "You can help me find out what's on the exam so I can get prepared beforehand."

"What?" Mom asked, as though she wasn't getting what I was saying.

"You can go and steal a look at the exam paper," I finally said, jarred a bit by the audacity of my suggestion.

Mom was taken aback: "How could you get such an idea?" she said. "That would be cheating!"

"I have been working very hard in preparing for the exam and have stayed up so many nights," I said. "Others who have spent no more time on this than me may pass the exam with flying colors. That's not fair."

"It's a matter of luck," Mom said. "It all depends on how lucky you are. It's a bit like the fairies. Some want to become a human, but if they can't feel deep affection for a real human, they can never gain enough weight to be a human and they have to float around the streets, night after night. That's also luck."

I wasn't interested in fairy tales at the moment.

Mom hugged me and stopped talking.

The night began to fall and tree leaves were rustling outside the windows. Sitting in Mom's arms, I felt so sad. Mom was gently scratching my back.

Then, abruptly, Mom patted me and said, "Okay! I will take you on another flight."

She had me put on a grey coat of hers so that people wouldn't easily spot us in the dusk. We wouldn't want people to see us flying around. Mom then had me climb on her back, and together, we jumped out of the third-floor window. I was scared and let out a yelp. By that time, Mom's body became invisible and I could only feel her warmth. I felt like I was jumping out a window into the unknown in a dream.

"Miao, don't clutch my neck so tightly," Mom whispered. "I can't breathe. Don't worry. I won't let you fall."

We were flying past the tops of plane trees. Below, I saw the policeman at Nanjing Road intersection. He, of course, didn't see me. He was busy scolding a motorist who had jumped a red light.

The street was packed with people getting off work. But none of them looked into the sky. So, no one saw a child flying above them. The neon lights on Nanjing Road suddenly came on and I saw a traffic jam. Motorcyclists were weaving across lanes and between vehicles. Many women squeezed into a delicatessen, probably too tired to cook dinner tonight.

In front of the Portman Hotel, a wide avenue stretched. There were no trees. A boy standing at the door of the Hard Rock restaurant looked up and saw me. His jaw dropped. Pointing at me, he couldn't find words. I stretched out my arms and made a flap like a little bird, hoping that the boy would think I flying all by myself.

"Don't do that!" Mom yelled. "You will fall."

Her voice was so loud that the boy below heard it. He looked around haplessly, trying to trace the voice.

But we flew on.

We came to Hilton Hotel. Many vendors were lined up along the adjacent streets, selling socks, buttons, hair clips, paintings, gardenia flowers and brush pens. Some dark, thin migrants were squatting there hawking old porcelain bowls and flasks. Mom whispered to me that they were selling fake antiques.

Then suddenly I saw Dad, briefcase under his arm, walking up from the Bus 49 stop. A lock of hair stuck up at the back of his head. He looked no different from all the other men walking home along the street.

Dad walked to a peddler selling brush pens and calligraphy copybooks. The man greeted Dad with a smile: "Teacher Chen," I heard the man say. Dad was never a teacher. I suddenly felt my gut tighten. Had Dad deceived me?

Dad took a large bundle of brush pens and copybooks from the peddler and gave him 100 yuan.

Mom said that man was Heavenly King's father. In order to pay the fees for his child's tutor, he peddled goods on the street after work. By buying goods off him, my parents were reimbursing him, in part, for our eavesdropping on the lessons.

Mom and I flew over his head but he didn't see us.

That night, back at home, Mom walked into my room and touched my face. She asked: "Feel okay?"

"Yes," I said: "Mom, kiss me."

She kissed me and whispered to my ear, "Now there is a lot of glue in my heart."

I looked at her cast in the light from my little red desk lamp. She had a beautiful smile. Although she liked the daytime sunshine because the fairies didn't have sun in their world, she always looked fresher and livelier at night.

"If I really mess up the exam, what will happen?" I asked.

Mom replied, "You have a heart filled with good feelings, which is the most precious thing in the world. If you pass the exam, that's good. If you fail, it won't be so bad."

"But others won't look it this way," I said. Feelings were nothing. Everyone had them. We needed more than that to have a good life.

Reading my thoughts, Mom whispered, "You human expect too much."

The next day at school the exam paper were handed out. After so many weeks worrying about this moment, I suddenly felt at peace with myself. The fear has disappeared.

Teacher Liu was right. The composition was about people.

After the exam was over, Mom picked me up from school and took me to Kentucky Fried Chicken. Many kids were there, accompanied by their parents.

"Are you happy?" Mom asked, as she sat across the table from me and the smell of warm chicken wafted throughout the room. "You have a happy expression on you face. I love the way you look just now."

Mom ate no chicken. She said it was too hot. She contented herself to drink Coke.

When we walked home, it was almost dark. The street lights were just coming on, and the plane trees cast eerie shadows across the sidewalks. People on the streets looked like moving ghosts.

"Ah, it's really good," Mom said, heaving a sigh of relief. She loved nightfall. She pulled her fingers one by one, making cracking noise. She did that to loosen up the bones from their fixed daytime positions.

Suddenly Mom touched me and said, "Miao, look at that person walking toward us."

I saw a grey-haired granny, short and thin but frisky. She wore a dark dress, and as we got closer, I noticed a big black mole on her forehead.

"She's also a fairy," Mom told me.

I was taken aback.

I never thought about other fairies walking the streets. Mom said fairies entering this world preferred dusk or dawn. Those were the times of day when they were most at home in two worlds.

Then Mom gave me another gentle touch and pointed to a child too young to be talking yet. He was sitting in his father's arms and he was crying even as he sucked on some candy. He also was a fairy, Mom told me. He had just arrived in this world and he missed home.

"When I first got here, I wanted to be a child, too," Mom said. "It's easier for kids to assimilate human feelings. But as soon as I saw your Dad, I knew that I wanted to live with him more than anything else."

Mom was indeed in love with Dad. That was comforting to me.

Seeing Mom, the child stopped crying. He had a

look in his face that you wouldn't see in a human child. It was as if he were saying, "I know you."

Mom smiled at him and reached out a hand to him. He was suddenly delighted and started laughing. His father began laughing, too. "At home, our child always cries in the evening," the man told Mom. "But once we are in the street, he sometimes unexpectedly smiles at some strangers."

Mom patted the child's hand. "He's a very smart little boy," she said. "You must love him very much."

The man held the boy tightly and said, "I'll do anything for him."

Tears suddenly welled in Mom's eyes.

That was the day I discovered that the streets weren't quite what I had always thought. There were actually fairies interspersed with us human. If you wanted to see them, you had to look at their shadows, which weren't as dark as those of humans.

I even saw a couple of young lovers walking close to us. Their hands were clasped. The young woman had a bluish shadow. Probably, Mom and Dad once walked along the street like this, I thought.

Just then, a Route 20 trolley bus pulled up at a red light next to us. Mom looked up and there was a person on the bus silently looking out the window at us. It was a young woman who resembled Mom.

Mom said nothing. I could see tears slowly appearing on the woman's face. One teardrop was quite big and it spilled out the open window of the tram. Mom stooped by the curb to catch it and when it touched her palm, it blossomed into a five-petal flower.

Mom told me that that woman was a fairy too and she was leaving for her home world.

"If I ever left this world," Mom said to me, with a poignant sadness in her voice, "you could come to this street at dusk and watch the fairies and think of me."

"Why would you want to go?" I asked.

"It's not that we want to go," she told me. "But sometimes, we have to go."

"Why?"

"Because we are not real human beings," she said. "I'm not saying that I will go. I was only musing."

I felt hollow inside. I knew what was going to happen. A vision came before my eyes. I saw our bathroom at home. There were only two tooth-brush mugs: Dad's and mine. Mom's red mug was still there but instead of a toothbrush, it contained only a single, white flower.

Slowly, my sight became blurry. Mom was walking just a step ahead of me, but I couldn't see her shadow at all. I began to cry.

I held on to Mom. She was real. You could touch her, warm. I put one of her hands on my shoulder and she hugged me. I loved Mom hugging me like that.

That day, I sensed that Mom could vanish at any moment.

I thought of Li Yuchen. She never told me how a home would be like without a mom. But she must have experienced the sorrow as I had at the moment. It's bigger than a lake, bigger than the sea and bigger than the sky. She could never swim out of that sorrow, because she could no longer live together with both her mom and dad. Also, once her father cited an excuse, she would be barred from staying alone with her mom at any time. In the world, nothing could be easier than asking an adult to find an excuse.

Chapter VI

Dad Presses for
a Divorce

It was Saturday morning and the sun crept across the floor to the legs of the table in the sitting room. On the table was a stack of white paper that Mom used for her illustrations.

It was 9:30. The big clock in the sitting room chimed. The Route 21 bus chugged down the street outside as it went past the traffic lights.

Dad and Mom were sitting at the table, both looking very serious.

"Chen Miaomiao, please come and sit with us," my father said.

I feared what he had to tell me. The exam was over and the matter of divorce again reared its ugly head.

"It's my fault," my mom said. "I shouldn't have come

to this world and shouldn't have had a child. I love you both but I can't change who I am and your father doesn't want to be married to a fairy."

My father nodded his head.

"What's wrong with Mom?" I asked. I didn't understand his feelings toward her.

He remained silent for a moment and then spoke with a heavy voice. "I just can't live with your Mom any more."

"How about me?" I asked.

"You must not be like Li Yuchen," Mom answered. "You must not forget to change your clothes when they are dirty. I have taught you many things and you must remember them all."

"Where will you go," I asked her, fighting back the tears.

"Back to my home world," she said.

I sat speechless.

"Originally, we planned to wait until you entered senior middle school to tell you about your mother," my father said. "But now you know. I'm glad that you aren't so afraid of her. I don't want you to hate your own mother. However, your feelings toward her can't substitute mine. I can assure you that I will always love you and don't want to hurt you."

If only I had not poured wine into Mom's cup! Seized with sorrow, I could find no words to say.

"Chen Miaomiao, I know it's difficult for you," he finally said, breaking the awkward silence. "You don't have to think too much about it now. Calm down and don't get agitated."

"What do you want me to do?" I asked.

"Nothing," he replied. "This is a matter between your mother and me."

I looked at him askance. How could it have nothing to do with me? My family was breaking up and I was going to end up motherless like Li Yuchen. I would have nightmares too. I didn't want to be like that, but I did not know what to do.

I walked around by myself for a while but my thoughts were too horrible to bear alone. So I decided to look for Li Yuchen.

Li Yuchen appeared on the second-storey balcony.

Her face, partly covered by her long hair, looked small and frail. I had never seen her like that before. She motioned me to come up.

Li Yuchen was home alone. Their apartment reeked of the foul smell of old radishes. If her mom had been here, the house wouldn't smell so bad, I thought to myself.

"What are you doing?" I asked, not wanting to launch into my miseries.

"Relishing sorrow at home," she said.

"Well, the exam grades haven't been announced yet," I said lamely.

We sat for a few moments in silence, and then without thinking I blurted out, "My parents are getting a divorce."

Li Yuchen's mouth dropped.

"What should I do?" I asked.

"Refuse to agree to it," she said. "Otherwise, you will end up like me. They say they are doing this to liberate themselves and you will be better off. But that's just selfish nonsense."

"How can I refuse to accept it," I said. "It's not me who is seeking a divorce."

Li Yuchen's eyes lit up. She said, "Of course you can do something. They will both ask you which one you want to live with, your mother or your father. You say that you don't want to live with either of them. You're not 16 yet, so you aren't allowed to live by yourself. That creates a dilemma that can't be resolved. And until it's resolved, there's no divorce."

Li Yuchen looked pleased with her own sagacity.

"I'd like to grow up and be a consultant specializing in help for children facing divorce in their families," she said. "I reckon that will be a booming business."

"Well, you have your first client," I said, pointing at myself.

Li Yuchen jumped from the chair eagerly. "Chen Miaomiao," she said, "you've come to the right person."

She went into her room and returned with a large scrapbook containing newspaper clippings she had collected about divorced families and kids with divorced parents. She said she had also bought a few books on the subject.

"Children are always the ultimate victims of divorce," she said, as she leafed through the pages. "Parents fall in love again. I think my mother is seeing someone. She is always dressing up like a young woman. But kids can never find a replacement for their own mother or father. I have thought this out. Kids are the ultimate victims."

Suddenly I felt a friendship with her deeper than I had ever before felt.

"I genuinely want to be your friend," I said.

"We are friends," she said. "I wasn't always sure of that in the past, but we are definitely friends now. You have a heart of gold, so you deserve a loyal and devoted friend. That's me. I'm that friend."

She began to tell me about the days of her parent's parting. She said she regretted that there were many things she should have done but had not. Perhaps the divorce could have been thwarted.

The newspaper stories she had collected repeated a common theme. Many children tried to manipulate the love each parent felt toward their offspring to mend the rift. Parents were often willing to sacrifice something for their children. "Other kids have done it, why not me?" Li Yuchen said she had asked herself over and over in the years after her parents' divorce.

But at the time, she had been timid and scared by the ferocity of her mother's anger at her father. So when the judge asked her with whom she wished to live, she pointed to her father.

Li Yuchen hit hard her forehead with her hand. "I'm the stupidest person in the world," she said.

So we decided to pull out all the stops, trying every strategy in her notebook.

We figured that I should fake illness because parents always rally to the cause when a child was sick. I could wash my hair and then stand in front of the air conditioners. Mom always said that was an invitation for a cold.

With that plot agreed, we parted company. On my way back home, I felt much better. I had an adviser now. I walked into the house vowing that I would be the catalyst for a happy reunion.

That night after Mom and Dad went to bed, I sneaked into the bathroom and wet my hair. I walked into the sitting room, where the air conditioner was. But as I passed my parent's room, I found their door unaccountably wide open. There was a small light in the room. Dad had unfolded the sofa bed and was lying there reading so intently that he didn't notice me. He was smoking and a bluish haze engulfed his head. Mom was asleep in the big bed. She didn't stir.

Since Dad was still awake, I didn't dare to turn on the air conditioner. So, I pretended to be going to the bathroom

Sitting on the toilet, I suddenly began to wonder about the open door. Had Dad done that intentionally because he wanted me to see that they no longer shared the same bed?

"It won't work," I murmured to myself with a certain glee.

If I couldn't catch cold, I would have to come up with something else. Dad was always saying the tap water was foul, so I filled up my toothbrush jug to the brim and gulped it down. Surely that would cause a bad stomach ache and diarrhea.

I lay in my bed, thinking that it had been such a long day. I fell asleep quickly and woke up again at midnight. No stomach ache. Maybe the tap water wasn't as germy as Dad always thought.

I perked up my ears and heard Dad snoring. I tiptoed into the sitting room. No one stirred.

I opened the little drawer of the dining table and found the remote control for the air conditioner. I took it out and clicked on the machine. A gust of cold wind blew into my face. I turned the temperature down as low as it would go. Then, I went into the bathroom to wet my hair. I rushed back to stand in front of the air conditioner, and in a few minutes I felt as cold as a popsicle.

I endured it as long as I could, then turned off the air conditioner and put back the remote. Before leaving the sitting room, I looked out the window at the street below. It was deserted. No people. No traffic. Even the policeman had gone home to sleep. The traffic signals had been turned to yellow blinking lights. I wondered if I might spot a thief in the night, but I saw no one.

I went back to bed. My still damp hair stuck to my face. Though I felt uncomfortable, I soon fell asleep.

The next morning, I awoke to bright sunshine. Dad was listening to the news on the radio. The newsreader said the Israelis and Palestinians were fighting again.

They were always fighting, I thought to myself. I touched my head and felt my belly. Nothing seemed out of the ordinary. Gosh, I thought, it's hard to get sick.

Mom walked into my room to tell me breakfast was ready. Seeing my hand on my forehead, she asked me if anything was wrong. "I thought I might have a fever," I said, trying to sound weak.

Mom said only a thermometer could tell if I had a fever and she went off to retrieve one from the bathroom.

A moment later, she was back, followed by Dad. She put the glass stick into my mouth and Dad stood beside me and held one of my hands to feel my pulse. Dad's hands were washed so clean and his nails were so white. He pressed his fingers into my wrist as if they were a stethoscope. I pretended to look innocent, but actually I was already feeling a bit guilty.

I had no fever and my pulse was normal, my father said.

"I felt a bit dizzy," I said.

"Of course, you have been working so hard on the exam," my mother said. "You need some rest."

"No," Dad said. "She should get up and move around. Sometimes, children tend to have low blood pressure in the morning, so they may feel dizzy. There's nothing to worry about."

I could do nothing but get up and act normally. But things were not normal in our household. We all sat at breakfast and said nothing. The lively conversations of the past seem to have dried up. I felt awkward in my own home.

Chapter VII
What Can Kids Do?

I went into the bathroom and locked the door behind me. Using the extension phone, I called Li Yuchen to report failure.

On the other end of the line, Li Yuchen let out a deep sigh. "Your body wasn't cooperating with our plan," she said.

I told her how the atmosphere in our home had turned strained. She said it was the same before her parents' divorce.

It was time to switch gears, she said. She suggested I say nice things about Dad in front of my Mom and nice things about her in front of him. I should buy flowers for Mom and tell her it was Dad's idea.

"I've seen this ploy work," said Li Yuchen, citing newspaper references. "All you need to supply are the white lies. You can lie, can't you?"

Of course, I could. Everyone could. So I agreed to try her new plan.

But I found the going tough. I had never been a honey-tongued speaker so I didn't know how to approach them without sounding silly. Not that they gave me much of an opportunity. The whole afternoon, Mom sat on the big bed and Dad sat on the sofa, like two rival armies in full battle position. They were talking in low voices and the door was shut. It seemed they weren't interested in my participation.

Hearing my movement in the sitting room, Dad called from the bedroom and asked me to join them if I wanted. "We have nothing to hide from you," he said as I opened the door.

"I'd rather not," I said and went out for a walk. It was really strange. In the past, I wanted to know what they were talking about. But now I didn't want to know.

That evening, Dad went to the hospital. Mom came over to me and gingerly touched my hand. "Miao," she said, "I know now the glue in your heart is uncomfortably sticky."

"Maybe, Dad has good intentions," I told her. "He

can get used to this situation. Time can heal things."

"Your father knew I was a fairy from the start," she said. "He has had plenty of time to get used to it."

"Is Dad a good man?" I suddenly blurted out.

What I wanted was to say some nice words about him in front of Mom, but I couldn't find them. Dad was the kind of person who would never do anything he thought was wrong. When I was younger, he carried me to school on his bike. When it was raining, I could smell his sweat from his warm back. Whenever Mom asked Dad to help her do something, Dad would immediately put down things in his hand and comply. When Mom turned blue that night, Dad panicked. A lot of scenes flashed back in my mind, but I couldn't say anything. It's not easy to say good things about your own father. So many of the cherished things were small and difficult to articulate.

"Yes, your Dad is the kind of man who suits the fairies best," my mother answered. "I told you before that there are only two kinds of people in this world who can hear us singing. They are the poets and the people with kind hearts like your father."

"That means you love Dad?" I asked.

Mom nodded. "I always remember the first time I saw him under the tree at the terminus of Bus Route 49," she said. "He was frowning. He carried a big black bag on his shoulder and stood there waiting for the bus. He was a medical intern then.

"By that time, I had been singing there for several nights. I had watched many people at the bus stop. Men looked around as if they were afraid of losing something or rather were hoping to find something on the ground. Some men always coughed loudly and spat. But your Dad's face was serene, unlike the rest.

"At that time, I was new here from my home world," my mother continued. "Fairies have nothing to grip. They keep floating around without any worries. I found it strange to see so many people looking preoccupied. Your father was handsome, a bit contemplative. Then, my heart began to grow heavy. The leaf that I was sitting on suddenly rustled. Your father raised his head, but he didn't see me, of course. I immediately blew a blue flower into his eyes. That way, he would become more inclined to fall in love with a fairy like me."

A trace of a smile appeared on her face. She was such a beauty.

Looking at Mom, I thought how nice it would be to fall in love like that. Love seemed very strange. It was hard to realize that these two people, who were once so much in love, now wanted to part.

"Why couldn't you continue to put the blue flowers into Dad's eyes?" I asked. "You could use your magic to rekindle Dad's heart."

"Your father's real love is already dead," she said sadly. "No matter how many blue flowers I put into his eyes, it won't help. Magic works for many things, but it can't really sway a man's heart."

"Do you still love Dad?" I asked.

Mom said, "I used to love him very much. But later on, when his love grew cold, my feelings changed. That's why a drop of wine now can turn me into blue. I have less and less things connecting me to human beings and am reverting back to being more and more a fairy."

"But Dad hasn't said anything bad about you," I said.

Mom nodded. "That's what makes him a better

man than most," she said. "He doesn't hate me. He just can't live with me."

It was all so complicated, this matter of personal feelings. I felt lost and confused. Mom suggested I should have a talk with Dad to try to understand his feelings. But by now, I was dog tired and wishing this whole time in my life was just a bad dream.

I felt powerless. Love was something I really didn't comprehend. I only knew that I loved my parents and they loved me. But they didn't love each other anymore, and that was the problem.

As I lay in bed that night, I recalled Li Yuchen telling me to buy flowers for my mother and telling her it was Dad's idea. But in my deep sense of discouragement, it seemed flowers wouldn't help much now.

I woke up refreshed and decided to try to work on Dad. He was the key to solving this family crisis. I decided to go to the terminus of Bus Route 49. That's where Dad transferred on his way to and from work, and it was also the spot where Mom and Dad first met. I wanted to have a look at that tree where Mom has rustled like a warm spirit, capturing my father's attention.

A Route 49 bus turned the corner at Jiangxi Road and rumbled into the terminus with a groan. There was a small island in the middle of the street, with some flowers growing in it. Vendors on the sidewalks peddled tea-flavored eggs and popsicles. An old man stood at the stop, his nose buried in a newspaper. An old lady nearby was doing exercises.

Behind the tree stood a red-brick church. That's the church Mom described. I walked over and tried to peer through the dust-covered windows. It was very dark inside. I wondered whether there were still some fairies living there.

As dusk began to fall, the street was packed with people getting off work. All kinds of cars and buses, many of them honking impatiently, filled the streets. I saw those same faces that Mom had described as heavy-hearted. They now looked unpleasant to me, too. When I grew up, I would never marry a person like that.

In the island garden in the middle of the street, a tree grew. I was a city child and didn't know tree names. It cast a big shadow over that little shed where the drivers of the Route 49 buses paused between runs to drink tea and wash their faces. That was the tree where the fairies sing. Each sat on a leaf. There had been no rain for some time, and I could see the leaves covered by a film of white dust. Would the clothing of the fairies be soiled?

I stood still and listened very carefully. Even despite the horns, the squeaking of tires, the peddlers' hawking and the policeman's whistles, I could hear the rustling of the leaves. Fairies must be there, I said. I wished I were a fairy, too.

Then I saw a man in the crowd, walking with his chin up as though he were swimming above the masses. Just as Mom had described it: a serene, clean face. If Mom could see this man, she would also like him, I thought to myself.

At that moment, I was startled to find myself staring into my dad's face.

He was startled, too. "What are you doing here?" he asked.

"Waiting for you," I answered meekly.

"Oh," Dad replied. "Maybe you know that this is the place where Mom and I first met. Mom told you, didn't she?"

I nodded.

"What else did she tell you?" Dad asked.

"She said she found you the most handsome and nicest man in the whole city," I said.

Dad laughed at that. "That's not quite true," he said. "Your mother had met few people. All one might say is that I am not a bad man."

"Mom says you are a super fine man and she loves you."

Dad said, "I know. She told me last night about some of the talks you two have had."

I was caught a bit off guard and not sure what to say. Dad led me to the small garden in the middle of the street and we sat down on a bench, staring across the road at the church.

"Miao, since that morning you said you had caught a cold, I have known that you are trying to do things to reconcile us. I have been touched by that. However, these are matters best left to your mother and me. This is not child's play."

I nodded.

"Your mother can't really change what she is," he

told me. "So it is me who has had to adapt. I am a surgeon working in a scientific environment where people don't believe in fairies. Of course I was taken aback to learn that your mother was a fairy. I will confess to you that I almost fainted.

"I read a lot of books about the subject, almost all psychological," he said. "Why? Because I wanted to accept this reality. I wanted science to help me accept it. Parapsychology talks about the existence of the soul, but it says nothing about feelings transposed to someone else. There is more to this than just flying around in the sky. You don't understand yet.

"I feel very remorseful," he said. "I have thought that it's not right for me to make the whole family so sad. So, I tried to love your Mom again. But it turned out that I couldn't do it. Love is very strange. If there's a person whom you cannot even touch, you can't really love that person."

"But you have never quarreled and when I was younger, I always thought you were very close."

"We could be very good movie actors," Dad smiled wryly.

"Now I know you are not happy," I said.

"It's loneliness," Dad said. "Very deep loneliness."

"Does that mean you have another woman?" I couldn't help myself from asking.

"There's no one else," he replied. "My heart is closed."

"So you can never be happy again unless Mom is gone?"

"I don't know whether I will be happy or not. At least, I can start a new life," Dad said.

"I can tell you that I'll be unhappy," I said. "I want both of you to live happily together with me."

"That's a very tall order," Dad said with a sigh. "To make you happy, I would have to resign myself to being unhappy."

"You should try," I said.

"Feeling is not an object," he said. "It's not something you can go out to buy like pencil and paper. Feelings are like water; once spilt, they are dispersed and you can't recover them."

We sat without a word for a few minutes. Finally Dad said, "It's very likely that I have hurt you because I'm selfish."

He lowered his head and after another long pause, said, "But I really don't want to live such a lonely life any more."

There was a sadness in his eyes. All of a sudden, I wanted to cry.

In the tree above our heads, there was the faint sound of singing among the rustling leaves. But the music was also full of sadness.

Li Yuchen sat at the table in her home, staring at me. After a long while, she said, "Then why did they bring us into this world? We did not necessarily want to come to this world, and it's them who have brought us here. They must take the responsibility for us."

I replied, "It's not that they don't want us. They don't hate us. It's only they themselves want to part."

But as I looked at Li Yuchen I knew I was looking at myself in the future and it was hard to remain even a reluctant defender of my parents' decision.

"Okay," she said, "Let's stop talking trash. We still need to concentrate on your parents. I like your mom a lot. She's a good person. The problem is your father."

"My Dad is also a good person," I had to say. "He's an honest man."

"Honest perhaps," she said. "Otherwise, he wouldn't have told you that he wanted to marry again. Under such circumstances, he can still talk straight, so he can be counted as an honest man."

I said: "Li Yuchen, you talk like a grownup."

She nodded: "I'm a grownup. All kids become grownups when their parents get divorced."

Chapter VIII

It's Not Easy to Become a Delinquent

For several days there was no more mention of divorce in our home. In fact, things had returned to some semblance of normalcy. But Li Yuchen said I should not be deceived. Her parents, too, had stopped talking about divorce. And the next thing she knew, she was hauled before a judge and asked which parent she chose to live with. By then, it was too late.

"Everything is not over until your dad personally tells you there will be no divorce," she counseled me.

Li Yuchen had another plan. She pulled out her scrapbook of newspaper clippings and showed me stories about how the children of divorced parents often go bad.

There was the female singer who began to take drugs. There was a boy who turned to crime.

"You know what I fear the most?" Li Yuchen asked me.

I shook my head.

"I'm fearing that I could go bad," she said. "I don't want to. Bad children have no future. What I fear the most is that I will unwittingly go bad."

Li Yuchen pressed her lips tightly together and looked at me with a grieved expression. Her eyes moistened but then she seemed to be talking to herself and she fought back tears before a single drop was shed.

"Li Yuchen," I said, "I believe that you are a good person and always will be. You have so much self-discipline."

She waved my words aside and moved closer. What my parents would fear most was that I might turn bad if they divorced, so I was to start acting like a rascal.

"How do I become bad?" I asked her. "Smoking? Swearing? Staying out late?"

I began to laugh. I had never done anything like that before, but the very ideas sounded a bit thrilling.

Li Yuchen said, "Yes, all these things. And you must dress up. The newspapers said that one of the signs of girls turning bad is that they suddenly begin wearing bizarre dresses."

We began talking about how to do bad things because this was all new to us. We talked until Li Yuchen's father came home from work. He changed into slippers in the doorway and threw his briefcase to the floor: "Oh, your little friend's here."

He gave Li Yuchen 30 yuan and told her to go out and eat noodles for supper.

"How about you?" Li Yuchen said, taking the money. "Do you want me to bring back some food for you?"

"I must lie down for a while. I'm dog tired," her father said.

Li Yuchen whispered to me, "He says that whenever he has a date with a woman and he's too embarrassed to tell me."

Li Yuchen and I left. It was dusk and the street was crowded with people heading home. We passed by a night club. A tall young woman stood under the lights, wearing a bright red qipao. She was smiling with what looked like a frozen expression. I often passed by this place during the day and the door was always closed tightly. I never knew what people did inside.

I said, "It's getting dark. I'd better get home."

"First have some noodles with me," she said. "I'll buy cheap ones and 30 yuan will be enough for two bowls."

I said, "My mom will be worried."

Li Yuchen smiled. "That's the whole point of being bad. You have to break the rules," she said.

My mentor and I found a table which was soiled. "They didn't wipe it clean," said Li Yuchen. "Don't put your hands on it."

The noodle shop was crowded but we were the only kids there without parents. I looked at the tables with families. They were ordering a whole range of dishes and they looked so happy.

I turned away and asked Li Yuchen, "I have to learn to use curse words. I've never done that before."

"Me neither," she replied.

"Shall we try?" I asked, hesitating but nonetheless excited.

Li Yuchen fought back a laugh and assumed a stony face.

"So, let's try," she said.

She looked at me, opened her mouth, but failed to utter a sound.

"You go first," she said.

I couldn't utter anything either.

"OK, let's be bold and try it together," she said. "One, two, three!"

"F - u -"

The tone of our whispery voices sounded as we were calling "Mo - m -", the bleat of infants.

My heart skipped a beat. I didn't know what to do but began to laugh.

Li Yuchen began to laugh, too. The two of us burst into loud laughter, causing a little pot of vinegar to spill onto the table.

A family with a young girl sat at the next table. The mother shot us a glare. Our noisy behavior must have been jarring.

Li Yuchen purposely laughed louder until her face turned deep red. She took a chopstick, dipped it into the vinegar and sucked on it. Then she pointed the chopstick at me and said, "Chen Miaomiao, you must not become too bad."

"I won't," I said.

The bowls of noodles were served. All this plotting and talking had made me hungry, so I chewed down the food.

On the way home, we bought a pack of cigarettes at a small shop. The man in the shop looked at us with a curious expression, but he didn't say anything.

I had never been out so late without telling anyone where I was. I knew Mom would be worried and I urged Li Yuchen to hurry. When we arrived at our building, I saw Mom standing on the balcony. She spotted me and waved.

When I got inside, Mom didn't scold me. "Wash you hands and get ready for supper," she said.

In the dim hallway light, Mom's face looked pale. Her hair, often done up in an elaborate bun topped with a crown, was pulled back into a simple ponytail. She looked sad and I didn't have the heart to tell her I had already eaten with Li Yuchen. So, I washed my hands and sat down at the table. But I had no appetite.

No one said anything. Dad ate little. Mom ate little. The room was so quiet that had any of us clinked a spoon against a bowl, the sound would have reverberated throughout the room. I tried to eat but my swallows caught in my throat. I dared not look up. After supper, Mom stood up to clean the table.

"If both of you feel fine, I can do anything. I can go back to my home world. It's easy, really. Fairies are born without feelings, so I won't feel as sad as you."

Mom had a smile on her face. I could not tell whether her comments were genuine or fake.

Dad looked at me and I looked at him. Neither of us said a word. Li Yuchen was right. The problem had boiled down to Dad and me. We were both selfish and stubborn.

The next night, in the bathroom, I smoked the first cigarette in my life. It made whole of my mouth taste bitter and it stank. I really couldn't figure why people liked smoking. My timing, just before Dad got home, was intentional. He always washed his hands first thing when he got home and he was certain to smell the foul air. I felt a bit scared. I didn't inhale the smoke. I just held it in my mouth and blew it out. It was quite strange to see smoke billowing out from my mouth as if I were a dragon.

The minute Dad stepped into the house, he began sniffing the air He first went into the kitchen to see if anything were burning there. Then he went into the sitting room and finally to my room. Although I wasn't afraid, my heart started to pound wildly in my chest.

"What are you doing?" he asked sternly.

I kept silent.

"Were you smoking?" he asked.

I still kept silent. Originally, I had planned to say, "It's you who is forcing me to this." But I didn't dare say anything as we confronted one another.

"Are you looking for a spanking?"

I began to cry, but I kept the sound of my crying low. Both Dad and I were afraid that Mom would hear it. We didn't want her to feel sad.

Dad reached out a hand to me. I took the pack of

cigarettes from the drawer and handed it to him. He used two hands to crumple the pack and walked out.

Then, I heard the toilet flush.

I felt very depressed. But since I had embarked on this plan, I couldn't just give it up at the first turn.

A few days later, when Mom wasn't home, I asked Dad for some money.

He looked at me bewildered, unused to my being so brazen.

He put down the newspaper and sat up straight. "What for?" he asked.

"Buying clothes," I said.

"Buying what kind of clothes?" he asked.

"The clothes that I prefer," I said.

"Your mother buys clothes for you," he replied.

"Mother is leaving us, so I need to buy clothes by myself," I answered.

He looked at me in silence, then nodded. "Okay," he said, "I will give you money to buy clothes."

He fished out a 100 yuan note from his pocket and gave it to me.

"100 yuan is not enough," I said.

Dad didn't say anything, then he recovered his composure with a faint smile.

"All right. Times are different," he said. "Kids nowadays wear expensive clothes. I will give you another 300 yuan. That's the same amount you donated to the Hope Project child at school last year. You can spend that for yourself."

I held the money in my hand and shot a look at Dad. He stared back at me with no expression.

Li Yuchen and I walked down Nanjing Road. We bought a small black vest and black jeans like those worn by foreign singers we saw on the TV music channel. In a small accessory shop, we bought a ring, but my fingers were too thin and it kept slipping off. So the shopgirl found a leather cord for me, the kind that some boys wore as necklaces. "You can wear the ring as a pendant," she said. "It's cool."

She herself was pretty "cool", decked out in silver lipstick that made her look like a cat. She also suggested we buy a pair of platform shoes. She said we should walk with our toes pointing like kids who had rickets. She said that's the latest fad.

Back at Li Yuchen's home, I put on all the new apparel. Because I was really thin, the vest and jeans made me look like a dried vegetable.

I went home, expecting to cause a stir when I walked in. Mom was sitting straight in a chair, and in one of her eyes was a blue flower and above her an eyeball that followed me like a little butterfly. Mom came over to hug me but she didn't say a word.

Dad looked at me and laughed. "Well, that get-up sure saves a lot of fabric," he said.

I was angry.

That night, when they were both in their room, I heard Mom say, "Love and hate are the same. It's the glue that comes out only from human hearts and it binds people together."

Perhaps to show their resolution not to reconcile, my parents had begun leaving their bedroom door open every night. It made it easy to hear what they said.

"Then what do you want me to say?" my father was asking her. "Adults and children can't really understand each other."

"She has her reasons," Mom told him.

As the final part of our plan to refashion me as a delinquent, Li Yuchen and I decided to stay out all night. I didn't dare to do it myself. We left one dusk, wandering the street without knowing what to do or where to go.

The neon lights on Nanjing Road flickered to life. Although people were scattering in all directions, it was obvious that most of them were going home. They carried vegetables, meat and fruit for supper, or bought roasted duck and chicken from the hooks hanging in delicatessen windows. Some were buying cakes and other pastry for tomorrow's breakfast.

I felt a bit antsy. When everyone's gone home and the streets turned empty, what then? What should we do if we bumped into some real rascals? Or murderers?

We decided we should stay in places that were brightly lit. First, we went to a Kentucky Fried Chicken shop. But the shop would shut at midnight so we couldn't stay there all night. Then, we wandered to a café that didn't close until 4 am. Looking through the big glass window, we could see the tables were covered with checked table cloth. On each table was a small candle. It looked very romantic.

Li Yuchen said it would be starting to get light after 4 am, so there was nothing to fear. But as we tried to enter the café, the proprietor waved us away. Kids under 18 weren't allowed in, he said.

Li Yuchen wasn't about to give up easily. "We just come to see if you really close at 4," she said.

The man wore a carefully ironed shirt. He was very fat and his hair was all combed toward the back of his head. He looked like a Mafioso in a Japanese movie. He was a bit intimidating.

I touched Li Yuchen, trying to urge her to go away. I had a feeling this wasn't the kind of place we wanted to park.

Li Yuchen whispered to me, "We should never let them see we scared." Then she said loudly: "We don't have to come here."

As we turned to leave, the man stopped us. "Come, come here," he said. On one of his thick fingers, he wore a large diamond ring. He smelled of cologne.

"Why do you two kids want to know when we close?" he asked.

"We are doing part of our sociology studies," Li Yuchen replied in an answer that impressed me.

The man let out a laugh: "Aha! Nowadays, kids even learn how to patronize café bars."

As we spoke, a young lady came over carrying a cup. She was wearing a red T-shirt and a baseball cap. She pressed her lips together and grinned at us: "What college are you from?" she asked.

I knew she was making fun of us.

"Maybe you quarreled with your parents and now you are trying to stay out all night," the man suddenly said, staring at Li Yuchen.

"That's not true," I retorted angrily.

That young lady patted on us on the shoulders and said: "Okay, now hurry home. This is not a place for young girls. It's already dark outside. You could run into some real bad guys."

The man at the counter poured each of us a cup of water and pushed them in front of us.

"You should hurry home," he said. "Young girls are

often the target of human smugglers."

Although dressed like a bad guy in the movies, this man turned to be kind-hearted if a bit pedantic. We sat on the tall bar stools drinking the water as he kept talking.

"I tell you, girlie, it's difficult to learn to be good," he said. "To learn to be bad takes less than a minute. But I can tell that you haven't given up on whatever it is you are up to. But if you run into trouble, dial 110 and ask the police for help."

We had begun to like this café very much but it was obvious we weren't welcome. So we left, traveling out in pitch dark now. I felt hungry and missed home, but I felt too ashamed to say it.

"Let's find a place to eat first," Li Yuchen said. "When we sit down eating, we will come up with some good ideas."

We went into a Yonghe Soybean Milk shop where we ordered fried dough sticks. To our surprise, we discovered that the shop was open 24 hours a day. It suited us very well. Brightly lit, full of people. The waitresses all looked young and jovial. No one would make a fuss about two young girls occupying a table for hours.

Best of all, there was a television set over our heads and "Growing Pains" was on. This was what one might call sticking it out and winning.

It was only 7 pm. We were content to eat a meal and watch the television. No one interfered. Then it was 8 pm and then 9 pm. We watched television, elated at the success of our plan.

Ten o'clock and eleven o'clock. We drank more iced soybean milk as drowsiness set in.

By midnight, Li Yuchen's eyelids were beginning to droop. But she held on. Finally, her eyes became as red as a rabbit's. She tried hard to keep them open and said to me, "Chen Miaomiao, I know how bad you feel. That's why I won't let you take this on by yourself. We are friends and we should share happiness and woes."

I gave her a heavy pat of affection, which she returned.

But then the going got tough. We bent over the table and fell asleep. Soon, our feet tingled. It was very uncomfortable. I looked into the street through the window and I saw a taxi with a red light cruising around, though I couldn't see a soul in the street. There was a bluish haze floating across the middle of the road.

It was past one o'clock in the morning when one of the waitresses roused us and suggested we go home. I must admit the idea sounded good to me, but it was so dark outside that we didn't dare venture forth.

"We are afraid to go out," I said.

The waitress called 110, asking police to take us home. Before we could figure out what to say to the police, two uniformed officers were there.

"These two kids are lost," the waitress told them. "Can you see that they get home?"

In no time, we were back in our neighborhood. One policeman walked me to my building and went into the concierge's office. Upon seeing me, the concierge, whom we called Fat Aunty, yelled out, "Where have you been? Your dad and mom have been so worried about you. They have been looking for you everywhere, and your mother's in tears."

As it happened, Dad and Mom weren't home. They were at the police station.

I should have said something, but I couldn't think what to say. I was nearly asleep, standing upright.

The next thing I knew, my parents arrived. Mom hugged me tightly. Dad said nothing. After thanking the policeman profusely, they marched me upstairs.

"Chen Miaomiao, you listen carefully," my father said. "You stop what you are doing, I will never say another word about divorce. I promise I will never mention it again."

I suddenly felt wide awake. I had won! Li Yuchen and I had won! It would be a good night's sleep ahead now.

Chapter IX
Something Earthshaking Happened Again

Outwardly, life in our household seemed to return to normal, back to the time before Mom drank wine and turned blue.

Li Yuchen admired me for having staved off a divorce and began writing a book for kids facing a split-up of their families. She planned to title the book "How to Stop the Divorce of Your Parents" and she said she wanted to use my experience as one case history because it had been so successful.

But there was still one unsettling reminder of the ordeal I had been through. Mom and Dad never closed their bedroom door as they once had, so I could see that Dad was still sleeping on the sofa and my parents weren't the loving couple I had once supposed. They were not happy together, but they were not going to get divorced.

To be honest, Dad was acting a bit differently. In the past, he had always read psychology books. Now, whenever he was home, he watched VCDs. At beginning, he bought them from a small shop in the street, one every day. Gradually, he gathered a boxful. All the VCDs were about war. Every night, he watched one new one and one old one for a second time. After that, he took a shower and went to bed. He treated both Mom and me very kindly, just as he always had.

One night, he rummaged through his box of VCDs for a long while, unable to find one that he hadn't seen at least twice. Then he called the shop, where he had become friendly with the shop owner, who would sometimes deliver the VCDs to the house.

That night, soon after Dad hung up, a man appeared at our door with a large bag on his shoulder. He looked like the salesman who peddled some kind of new dishwashing cloth door-by-door in our apartment block. Dad and the delivery man dumped all the VCDs from the bag on the floor and checked them one by one. Dad still couldn't find a war movie that he hadn't watched already. Sometimes, I watched the movies with Dad. I had become quite familiar with the Korean War, the Vietnam War, and the European wars.

That night, after the delivery man left, Dad turned the VCD box upside down once again and finally picked a film to watch. It was a very gory war movie and the scenes of people bleeding unsettled me.

Dad buried himself in the sofa, motionless. American soldiers threw daggers at the Vietnamese. The Vietnamese, in turn, sharpened the ends of bamboo poles as weapons to kill the Americans. "Close your eyes, Chen Miaomiao," Dad used to tell me, whenever something came on the screen he didn't think I should watch. But he didn't this time.

I turned my head away, but when I later cast an eye back on Dad, he was fast asleep. His face was etched by two deep lines from his nose to his mouth. His mouth, puckered, looked as if he had just taken some bitter medicine. For the first time, he looked old and pained to me. That wasn't how I had always known him. He has lost his talkative, active nature and his sense of humor was gone.

The wrenching screams of people in the movie didn't wake him. Dad's head was tossed back and his arms dangled from the sofa rests. Only his hands hadn't changed. They were still the immaculately clean tools of a surgeon.

Had Dad changed so much because his plans for divorce had been stymied?

As I later lay in bed that night, the question kept coming back to me. I remembered the times when I was denied something I wanted badly and how I had felt. Poor Dad. There must have been pain in his heart. However his grief, he bore it in silence. He seemed to be melting away from me and Mom, like ice cream on a hot day.

I discussed it with Li Yuchen. "You're feeling sorry for your dad," she said.

I knew she was right. I recalled how Mom, too, often watched Dad from behind and something like tears glistened in her eyes. I believed she, too, felt heartache for him. She was talking to me one day while working on an illustration for a newspaper. She drew a flock of little birds flying in a line. Then she began to cry. A teardrop fell on the paper, blurring the ink. Mom used a piece of issue to absorb the water and then turned the blurred ink into a moon floating through a cloud.

I told Li Yuchen that I was confused. Mom and I found no joy in our triumph over the divorce. No one in our home was happy.

"I didn't expect that either," Li Yuchen told me. "What we wanted most was to see all of you live together happily. We didn't intend to hurt anyone, did we? Everyone in your family has a heart of gold. I don't know why your father so badly wants a divorce. I don't understand it."

At that point, I couldn't hold it any more.

"If you swear not to tell anyone else, I'll tell you a reason that Dad can do nothing to change," I said.

She promised to keep the secret.

I took a deep breath. "My Dad doesn't want to stay married to my Mom because she's a fairy," I said. "They don't even share the same bed anymore."

"Fairy?" Li Yuchen said. "Fairy? What do you mean by fairy?"

"She is not a human being like we are," I said. "She is a fairy."

Li Yuchen's mouth dropped and for a moment she was speechless.

"Does she eat humans?" she asked.

"No."

"Does she have a long, bloody red tongue and sharp teeth?"

"No."

"Then I don't know what you mean by fairy," she said, looking at me as though she might suspect I had lost my mind.

I told her about some of the fantastic things Mom had done and how she had helped me in ways no one else could.

"Your dad is really stupid," she finally said. "Your Mom is great. Please ask her to take me flying sometime. I swear I won't tell anyone."

She suddenly stopped and stared at me a moment.

"Are you a human or a fairy?" she asked.

"I'm human," I replied, somewhat indignant that she should ask. "My Mom told me I'm human. I'm too heavy to fly."

Li Yuchen looked at my mouth and said suspiciously, "But your two incisor teeth are quite sharp, I notice."

She got up and went to the kitchen, returning with some cooking wine. She motioned me to drink a little of it. I took a swallow. It was bitter and pungent. We waited for a few moments, but I didn't turn blue.

"That's disappointing," she said.

"That's just what I think," I said. I really wished I were a fairy like Mom.

That was the day that cemented my strong friendship with Li Yuchen. We had shared hardships and now we shared a very special secret. We had grown up a bit and weren't the children we once were.

When the sadness in our home lifted, I would ask Mom to take Li Yuchen flying, I told myself. It was the least I could do for such a trusting good friend.

When I got home, Dad was in earlier than usual. He sat at the table helping Mom prepare dumplings.

Dumplings stuffed with prawns was a special treat she sometimes prepared in summer.

It warmed my heart to see the two of them sitting together at the table. I didn't dare utter a sound because I was afraid I would break the spell of the moment. I stood at the door, just gazing at them. A cool breeze swept past me, blowing over them like a lilting piece of silk. I looked at Mom's white sandals sitting next to Dad's black leather shoes. I had never really look at my home through those eyes. It looked so good to me.

I prayed to God, Kwan-yin, Buddha, Allah and any gods that existed in heaven for Mom and Dad to become a loving couple again and for us all to live happily ever after, just like in fairy tales.

I went to bed that night in an airy mood, hoping that perhaps some magical force would put everything back right in our home. But then came another earthshaking revelation.

In the middle of the night, I woke up and climbed out of the bed to go to the bathroom. It was very quiet. A big, bright moon shone through the window, bright as the sun, casting a long shadow across the room. A water drop hanging from the faucet glistened like a diamond in the moonlight.

Then I heard a strange sound. I thought it might be coming from the street, so I ran to the window. The street outside was empty. A group of pigeons was roosting on the roof of the opposite building. At the sight of me, they took wing and began flying around outside our window. The sound of their beating wings was somehow ominous.

I walked through the apartment, smelling something odd. At first I couldn't place what it was, but then it reminded me of the scent when my baby teeth had fallen out of my mouth, causing some bleeding. It was the smell of blood! Fresh and pungent.

I followed the source of the smell to our pantry, where a yellow light shone through the keyhole. I peeped through.

There was Mom, all blue, squatting on the ground with a scalpel in one hand and a little green animal tightly gripped in another. It was a little frog and it was bleeding. The blood dripped into a blue bowl. Mom was killing a little frog, the little animal I loved the most. We used to keep tadpoles in the house but they had always disappeared mysteriously once they started to grow legs. They must had escaped because they knew otherwise Mom would kill them.

My heart shivered violently as I watched Mom raise the blue bowl to her mouth and drink the little frog's blood. She gagged after her first sip but that didn't stop her from drinking the bowl's full contents.

As she drank, her blue color gradually faded away and soon she was restored to her normal appearance. She put the frog's carcass into a box she had painted with angels and stars. I had seen her paint many of them over the years, but when I had inquired what they were for, she had said only that I was not to touch them because they were for special people.

Before Mom closed the box, she sobbed. She reached her hand into the box to touch the frog one last time and murmured, "I'm sorry, I'm sorry."

The pigeons that had been flying outside our window suddenly flew away.

I couldn't contain myself anymore and let out a

scream. Mom quickly tried to stand up and ran towards the door. I jumped aside then fled to the sitting room. Dad appeared and held me to try to calm me down.

"Don't be afraid," he said. "Don't be afraid. Mom has to do what she did. She has no other choice."

It was incredible. Dad knew all about this. He had known all along.

"I never had the heart to tell you," he said. "It's so cruel for a child to learn."

Then he sat down with me and tried to calmly explain how fairies like Mom came from a world without a sun. They wanted to live in the human's world, but it was hostile to them in some respects. So they frequently had to drink the coolest blood they could find to maintain their human appearances.

Then Dad confessed to me that when he had first learned of Mom's need to kill frogs and drink their blood, the idea of divorce first planted itself in his mind. He said life was like that. Sometimes things that seem so perfect have heart-breaking flaws.

Mom stood in the shadow of the sitting room.

"I'm sorry," she said in a mournful voice. "I don't want to scare you. I have to leave. I know that now. I have to leave both of you."

The next day, Mom and Dad filed for divorce. Li Yuchen came over to keep my company while they were gone. It was the first time she had ever been in our home and she looked around curiously.

"I don't see any signs of a fairy living here," she finally said. "A fairy who sleeps in a human bed, eats human food, wears human clothes and brushes her teeth hardly seems like a fairy at all. It's very strange."

Not long after, Mom and Dad returned. Mom recoiled momentarily when she saw Li Yuchen standing in our home. She looked at me and then looked at Li Yuchen: "Li Yuchen," she said, "Thank you for coming over to keep Chen Miaomiao company. You are such true friends. From now on I hope you spend more time together."

Mom looked at me, her eyes rimmed with kindness and sadness. I understood her sad expression now. She felt remorse about the terrible things she had to do in order to stay with us in our world. I couldn't bear to continue to gaze into her eyes. My heart ached at the thought of having to part with her forever.

Mom turned and clapped her hands. "Okay, everyone's here today," she announced cheerily. "Li Yuchen, will you join us for lunch?"

"Chen Miaomiao told me that your prawn dumplings are divine," Li Yuchen replied. "I'd like to have some."

We all crowded into the kitchen to help with the final preparation. Dad shelled the prawns and Li Yuchen and I prepared the veg for stuffing. Mom diced shallots, bamboo shoots and mushrooms. She searched for some ingredient on the top shelf of the cupboard, where she stored dried goods.

Dad touched Mom and said: "Too many tastes may offset one another."

Mom thought about it for a second and said: "Maybe, I should leave out the mushrooms. You have always said they don't go well with prawns."

Dad nodded. "We can use the mushroom to make a soybean soup," he suggested.

"That will be very tasty, too," Mom agreed.

Mom finally stirred some sesame oil into the stuffing. The whole house was filled with its fine aroma.

The four of us enjoyed a scrumptious meal together. Mom even allowed us kids to drink Coke because she said it was a special day. Li Yuchen ate so much that when she stood up she farted loudly. She instantly blushed.

Dad pretended he had heard nothing. Mom looked uncomfortable, then she simply smiled gently at Li Yuchen, who turned to me and said loudly, "What's that sound? What's that sound?"

Mom couldn't help but burst into laughter and so we were all laughing.

"That's all right," Dad finally said. "It's just a signal that Li Yuchen's digestive system is working properly."

That afternoon, Dad left for office. He said he would come home early that evening so we could see Mom off together. He patted me on my head before leaving but said nothing.

While helping Mom wash up the dishes, Li Yuchen took the opportunity to ask a lot of questions about fairies. I was in the sitting room, half listening to their voices. That gentle, silk-like breeze blew through the sitting room. I looked at Mom's white sandals in the hall. Soon they would be gone forever, along with her toothbrush. I would use her toothbrush mug for a flower vase in memory of her.

Li Yuchen and Mom walked into the sitting room, carrying plates of watermelon slices. I pretended to be asleep, causing them to lower their voices.

Mom told Li Yuchen that I always developed a rash on my legs in the winter and asked her to remind me to apply some Vaseline cream after taking a shower. While they talked, they tidied up the house cleaning the lamps, ironing Dad's shirts, dusting the shelves. Then, Mom pulled out a large suitcase from underneath the bed to show to Li Yuchen. It was full of my clothes. Mom had bought almost all the clothes I would need before I turned 18. There were also 100 pairs of stockings of different sizes.

I felt like crying, but how could someone who looked to be asleep cry? I tried to fight back my tears but the harder I tried the more they streamed down my face.

Chapter X
Goodbye Mom

It was dusk, Mom's last evening. She agreed to take Li Yuchen and me flying before she left. She held one of each of our hands and the three of us flew out the window.

Li Yuchen let out a cry of excitement and Mom shushed her, reminding both of us that we were not to let others hear us. But it was too late. That black-faced policeman at the crossroad heard a sound above his head and looked directly up as us. He covered himself with his arms and hands, as though he feared we would fall on him. Then he stood up straight and his mouth dropped when he realized we were flying, not jumping to our deaths.

Choo! Choo! Choo! He blew his whistle. Motorists on the road stopped, thinking the whistle was directed at them. The policeman pointed skyward to us. Choo! Choo! It was obvious he didn't know what to do. By now, all the cars and buses on busy Shaanxi Road had come to a halt.

Then, suddenly he recognized me. I was that little girl crossing the street everyday after school. We met before. When I was younger, he often came to take me across the road, simply because there were too many vehicles and I was so little. When I getting bigger, I became impatient and began to cross the street by weaving between vehicles. Standing in the middle of the crossroad, he yelled at me: "Are you looking for death?" When he yelled, his voice was much louder than the bombilation of all vehicles on Nanjing Road.

This time, he stared at me with wide eyes and yelled: "Are you looking for death? Get your ass down!"

He didn't understand it. This was flying, why should I get down.

Quickly we flew away, gliding along the tops of the plane trees that lined Nanjing Road. As we approached the Park Hotel, Mom took us higher and higher, afraid someone on the ground would spot us.

At that moment, we heard the voice of a small boy yelling, "Hello! Hello!"

We saw a blonde boy standing on a balcony of the top floor of the hotel. He was waving at us.

"Which of you is Peter Pan?" he yelled out to us.

Li Yuchen and I kept our mouths shut.

"Peter Pan is in England," Mom shouted down to the boy. "That's far away."

"Ah, that explains why I never saw him since I came to China," the little boy shouted back at us. "He promised to take me flying. Will you tell him I am counting on that when I get back home?"

"I'll will tell him that," Mom yelled back.

"And Tinker Bell, the little fairy. She always does something wrong, but I still forgive her because she has a kind heart. The first time when she was dying, I was too young. I didn't applaud for her because I hated her. That's why she didn't get much applause. Though survived, she's never been in good shape. Now, think about it, I feel kind of guilty. Please tell her, I'm sorry."

Mom answered: "She will understand and she will certainly feel ashamed for the wrong things she had done. She will believe you are an honest good kid and will never have ill feelings against you."

"You sure?" the boy asked gladly.

"Yes, you can have my word on it," Mom said seriously.

Solemnly, the boy nodded and said: "Thanks. I can't shake hands with you, 'cause I'm afraid of falling off. It's too high here."

Mom smiled: "That's OK. Be a good boy."

Then we flew away, with the small boy still waving at us.

It was getting darker and we saw lights blinking on below us. It was all very beautiful, the mixture of headlights on the roads and the flashing of neon. Nanjing Road was aflood with lights all the way down to the river. Further away we could see the bridges and the Oriental TV Tower. The city was so beautiful from a vantage point we had never seen before.

Flying across People's Square and the cobwebs of power and trolley bus lines on Fuzhou Road, we came to the stop of the Bus Route 49. It was still crowded with people heading home from work. A line of people waiting for the bus stretched along half the length of the road. Everyone looked grumpy.

We saw that big tree where Mom and Dad had met. Its leaves rustled in the wind and glistened in the lights.

"Abracadabra! I'm heading home soon," Mom said to no one in particular. "I'm taking my daughter and her best friend on a small trip beforehand. Please show yourselves to them."

The tree suddenly began to emit a blue ray. It took me a minute to see that the ray was being emitted from little blue beings sitting on the leaves. I couldn't see their faces clearly. Their shadows all were transparent.

People at the nearby bus stop were stunned by this sight. One man with slicked back hair and a big briefcase under his arm loudly told the people next to him, "Oh, it's just a laser show. Must be some company's advertising gimmick."

Someone hushed him. There was singing coming from the tree. I heard it, too. It was the sound of faint bells tinkling. And there were words, very faint words:

"I'm the blue person who longs for feelings,
Would you like to glue my heart?
I'm the blue person who has taken all the hardship,
Would you forgive my heart?

I'm the blue person who will inevitably leave,
Would you remember my heart?"

At that moment, a Route 49 bus turned from Jiangxi Road and its headlights cut apart the scene like two knives. Instantly, the tree dimmed and looked like just any other tree.

The man with oily hair said: "Not bad, which company's creative idea is that?"

We flew higher and away.

"After you leave, will you ever come back again?" Li Yuchen asked my mother. I knew she was asking on my behalf.

"No," Mom answered, "I won't be back."

She squeezed my hand as she spoke.

"Every fairy has only one chance to come to live in this world," she said sadly. "I have used mine. I've been here relatively long and lived well. Many fairies who come here end up hating humans and go home sad."

"Are you a sad fairy?" Li Yuchen asked.

"I'm not. But I will cry. I love the people I've met

from the bottom of my heart. I knew I wasn't suitable for this world, but I forced it upon myself. In the end, I hurt others for my own sake. I feel truly sorry in my heart. If there were another opportunity of coming to this world, I wouldn't take it."

She continued her melancholy words of farewell. "Fairies can turn themselves into cuckoos, singing all the time. But the city is not the place for them, so they live in woods in deep mountains."

I could find work in the future deep in the mountains where I might hear the cuckoos' song and think of Mom. The lights from the ground reflected on her beautiful face. If she turned into a bird, she would be the most beautiful one, I thought.

Mom turned and looked at me. "Human's life is beautiful," she said. "But if one can't get over sad things, one's heart will become too tired to beat. In one's life, you should always keep your heart pumping fast and high."

I knew that Mom wanted me to continue to be happy after she left. She had always said she loved putting her ear to my chest and hearing my heartbeat because she herself had no heart to beat

Mom was getting tired so she flew us home. She was waiting for the stroke of midnight for her departure. At that hour, a few minutes opened up when the human world and the fairy world were connected.

"Chen Miaomiao and I will see you off," Dad said.

"But you will feel uncomfortable," she said. "The fairy bus will come and some fairies will exit and some will get on. It will feel very cold to you."

Dad said we wouldn't mind. I nodded. Li Yuchen said she would like to be there, too.

Just before midnight, the four of us went out of our house. In the courtyard, a cat lurked under a big tree, its green eyes glistening from the lamp post light. It let out a whimper as though mourning Mom's departure.

The neon lights on Nanjing Road lit up a small bank of blue fog in the middle of the road. An almost empty trolley bus rumbled along, dispelling the blue fog. A white-haired old man sat next to a window on the bus, looking quietly at us. Suddenly, he reached out a hand, palm facing outside. Mom did the same toward him. I knew that old man must be a fairy, too. They must be saying good-bye to each other.

Mom led us into a back street. It was the street leading to Li Yuchen's home.

We walked straight all the way to Li Yuchen's apartment building. There was a large piece of empty land there where buildings had been razed for redevelopment. In the middle of the site was a lone island of high wild grasses. They looked white in the moonlight.

Despite the fact that it was summer and the day had been sweltering, we suddenly felt very cold. Li Yuchen began to shiver.

"Here we are," Mom said.

So, this was the fairies' bus stop. Mom looked around and sighed with satisfaction. "No other fairies here tonight," she said. "That's good."

Dad held me in his arms, and I looked at Mom's moonlit face. She looked tired but very pretty. I handed her an envelope. It contained photos that I had taken: dusk at the Route 49 bus stop, our sitting room, various family pictures. I hoped they would remind her of us when she was back in her fairy world.

She touched my face. Her hand was icy. "Chen Miaomiao," she said gently. "Chen Miaomiao, you are my very special girl. Thank you. Thank you for everything. Even without those photos, I would never forget you."

Dad moved to hug Mom but there was little to hold on to. She was already beginning to fade out. None of us had quite expected her to leave like this, bit by bit. We could still see her just in front of us, but we couldn't touch her any more. Dad didn't know what to do, so he kept murmuring to Mom as well to himself: "Don't worry. Don't worry. You shouldn't be too sad."

Mom's face gradually became blue in the moonlight and then was covered by a pale bluish haze. I could hardly make her out any more. "Mom! Mom!" I shouted.

I reached out to grab her, but her clothes slipped through my fingers like a shadow. I only caught a bit of blue. A big star overhead suddenly emitted a very bright light, softly wiping out the last bit of blue from my hand.

"Mom!"

Although there was no wind, the tall grasses rustled noisily. Then they suddenly parted in the middle, carving out a path. Deep in the middle of it was a small spot lit

142

white by the big star.

The blue shadow of Mom was fading out and then vanished like the haze in the street.

She was gone.

Small slips of paper floated out from the cluster of wild grasses, falling at our feet. They were the pictures I had given Mom, but now their edges were frayed and their images worn. Mom failed to bring a human present back to her home. She just returned it to me. But on every picture, she had stuck a little blue flower. Now they became the present Mom gave to me, to remind me of a childhood with a fairy mother.

Li Yuchen, who had been quiet throughout this farewell, broke into tears. Something dropped to the ground with a thud. It was a can of Coke Li Yuchen had planned to give Mom.

"Don't cry! Don't cry!" Dad said. "Otherwise fairies will leave with great pain. Please, don't cry!"

Li Yuchen covered her mouth with her hands.

Let my mom go home in peace. Don't cry.

(The End)